Cameron in Command

BY THE SAME AUTHOR

Featuring Lieutenant St Vincent Halfhyde, RN:
Beware, Beware the Bight of Benin
Halfhyde's Island
The Guns of Arrest
Halfhyde to the Narrows
Halfhyde for the Queen
Halfhyde Ordered South
Halfhyde and the Flag Captain
Halfhyde on Zanatu
Halfhyde Outward Bound

Featuring Donald Cameron:
Cameron in the Gap
Orders for Cameron

Cameron
in Command

Philip McCutchan

St. Martin's Press
New York

CAMERON IN COMMAND. Copyright © 1983 by Philip McCutchan. All
rights reserved. Printed in the United States of America. No part of
this book may be used or reproduced in any manner whatsoever without
written permission except in the case of brief quotations embodied in
critical articles or reviews. For information, address St. Martin's Press,
175 Fifth Avenue, New York, N.Y. 10010.

Library of Congress Cataloging in Publication Data

McCutchan, Philip, 1920-
    Cameron in command.

    1. World War, 1939-1945—Fiction. I. Title.
PR6063.A167C27 1984   823'.914   83-26881
ISBN 0-312-11446-X

First published in Great Britain in 1983 by Arthur Barker Limited.

First U.S. Edition

10 9 8 7 6 5 4 3 2 1

Cameron in Command

1

THE sky was dull and heavy; greyness lay over all. Grey sea heaved along the corvette's sides – big waves with little in the way of wind to take spray from their tops. It was a swell left behind by a recent gale. The little warship lifted and plunged sickeningly, swooping like a bird down the walls of solid water, climbing up the other side to hang poised for a while before beginning another slide. There was no land in sight; and when land came up it would be an uninspiring coastline with much danger behind it. The tip of South America, not so far north of Cape Horn with its continual westerlies, was an iron-hard place for any seaman.

Cameron stared from his bridge into the gloomy wastes, head sunk on to folded arms on the fore guardrail but eyes nonetheless watchful. He heard the pipe along the deck below: Hands of the mess, muster for rum .... It was noon, and a bright moment for the ship's company in a day of heave and wetness and general discomfort. On the heels of the pipe there was a clatter of feet on the ladder behind. Cameron turned, to be saluted by a sub-lieutenant arriving to take over from the forenoon watchkeeper. The sub was almost obscured in an oilskin over a duffel-coat and a flapping sou'wester that dripped with the rain.

'Morning, Sykes.'

'Good morning, sir.' Sub-Lieutenant Sykes sounded as weary as ever; he was a dull man at the best of times, Cameron thought, and not happy in his work. The war had brought him into the Navy from a comfortable rut buttressed by a wife and two children plus a semi in Twickenham, bought on a mortgage paid for by his comfortable job as second-in-command of a Woolworth's store. To become manager was his life's goal but war had intervened. Like Cameron himself, he had joined as an ordinary seaman but had only recently been commissioned as a sub-lieutenant RNVR, taking longer than was usual to get his recommendation. At thirty, he was old for his rank; age alone would soon bring him his second stripe. Not keenness or efficiency. Cameron frowned; Sykes didn't pull his weight and the ship's company, as well as their Captain, knew it. Although he had been in management, Sykes tended to be union minded and always had an eye for what he considered his rights. In Cameron's view, not good officer material. He should never have been given his belated recommendation. In the job that lay ahead of HM Corvette *Briar* every man would need to give of his best. Ninety-nine per cent of them would.

Cameron turned to face for'ard again, stared out at the eternal South Atlantic across the 4-inch anti-aircraft gun on the fo'c'sle, over the heads of the huddled gun's crew in their wet-shiny oilskins, his mind ranging ahead of the ship as he tried to make assessments of every possibility, searching for some aspect that he might as yet have failed to consider. His first command had to be a success. He was very conscious of the brand-new half-stripe now sewn between the two wavy gold rings on the cuffs of his monkey-jacket hanging in his cabin, and on the shoulder-straps of the battledress blouse currently beneath his duffel-coat. Lieutenant-Commander Cameron, RNVR: there was satisfaction in that, but it had yet to be proved that he was equal to it.

And to command.

The Admiralty, at all events, hadn't seemed to be in any doubt. Reporting to the Second Sea Lord's office in Queen Anne's Mansions, Westminster, after a few months spent in a fill-in job in the Western Approaches after returning from Operation Torch, the seaborne British-American landings in North Africa, Cameron had been told of his accelerated promotion.

'For services rendered during your time in the Med,' a Captain RN had told him with a smile, making it sound like another decoration to add to his DSC. 'You've been consistently well reported upon, Cameron. Fit for command and all that. Well, as it happens, we have a command for you.'

This was totally unexpected. Cameron stared. 'A command, sir?'

'Yes. Freetown, Sierra Leone – you've been there before, of course. I know you've done more than your share of foreign service . . . but Freetown has an urgent need of a commanding officer for a corvette, and you're experienced in corvettes by now – and you fill the bill. Do your best, Cameron – and the best of luck to you.'

The urgency, the Captain went on to say, lay in two things: firstly there was a hint of a special mission in the air, a mission that Cameron would learn about from the Flag Officer West Africa to whom he was to report immediately upon arrival on the station; and secondly the corvette's CO had died of yellow fever, one of the scourges of an area of West Africa that had not so long ago been known as the White Man's Grave. There was no local availability of a replacement; and Cameron would leave the UK next day, reporting to the naval base at Greenock on the Clyde for passage out in the battleship *Rodney*.

Fourteen days later he was sweltering in Freetown's rainy heat, sweating into his white Number Ten uniform when he reported to Rear-Admiral Pegram, Flag Officer West Africa, who lost no time in giving him his detailed orders.

'It's a tough operation, Cameron – very tough, very important. If I had a destroyer to spare, I'd use it, but I haven't. We're pushed to the limit with providing escorts for the WS convoys, patrolling for raiders and so on. It's asking a lot of a corvette – but there we are.' The Rear-Admiral paused. 'By the way, you've got a first-class Number One. If he'd had more seniority he might have been given command when Matthews died, but he's only just got his second stripe. Perhaps I ought to add he's RN, but don't let that scare you!'

Cameron didn't intend to let it scare him but knew that Pegram had passed a warning: it was seldom that professional RN officers were called upon to serve under RNVR command and they might not take too kindly to it. But Cameron intended to command his own ship from the start.

When, after leaving the Rear-Admiral's office, he went aboard the corvette, he found Humphrey Frome to be pleasant and friendly. 'Welcome aboard, sir,' the First Lieutenant said formally but with a smile.

Cameron shook his hand. 'Thank you, Number One.' He looked along the corvette's decks. 'She looks very smart.'

'First impression good, sir?'

Cameron grinned. 'Excellent!'

Frome looked pleased and relieved. The smartness of a ship was her First Lieutenant's responsibility, and first impressions counted. He introduced the other officers: an RNR sub-lieutenant named Morgan who had come from the Orient Line on the outbreak of war, a short, square young man with an air of confidence and authority; then Sykes and another RNVR sub named Thompson, and finally an RNVR midshipman with the faintly off-putting name of Carruthers, who confessed to having done nothing very much before he'd joined. Midshipman Carruthers had a somewhat languid air and seemed totally unserious and Cameron put him down as having a rich and indulgent father – something that he learned later was indeed the fact. Having thus met his officers, Cameron asked the First Lieutenant to come with him to his cabin. Once inside, he said, 'I have orders from the Rear-Admiral, Number One.'

'Yes, sir?'

'We go to sea after full dark tonight. I take it you're all ready?'

Frome nodded. 'I will be, by dark.'

'Stores, ammunition, fuel, water. Who's the navigator – Morgan?'

'Yes, sir. RNR ... Morgan's our most experienced seaman, more than me, I admit.'

Cameron nodded. 'Well, the Orient Line runs good ships. Morgan will have to know the orders, which I'm about to pass on to you. They're to go no further for the time being – understood, Number One?'

'Understood, sir.'

'Right.' Cameron took a deep breath. 'It's a long way. We're under orders for the Falklands in the first place. We'll take oil fuel and any other replenishments at Ascension, and we're to rendezvous with an RFA oiler between Ascension and the Falklands to top up again at sea.'

'Hazardous . . .'

'So is war, Number One. In Port Stanley we embark a demolition party of Royal Engineers and then we leave for the channels north of Cape Horn. That takes us into shared Chilean and Argentinian waters – neutral waters.'

'That's hazardous, too,' Frome said. 'What are the locals expected to do about us?'

Cameron shrugged. 'Not see us, for preference! That part we'll have to play by ear, take it as it comes.'

'What's it all in aid of?' Frome looked puzzled.

Cameron said, 'Remember this is very highly classified information, Number One. The fact is that the Japs are expected to attempt a landing on the Falklands – the *Birmingham* and the armed merchant cruiser *Asturias* have been sent in as some sort of protection, but we all know that an AMC like the *Asturias* can be sunk by just one broadside and it's not thought to be enough – '

'And no more ships can be spared?'

Cameron nodded. 'Right. So the Admiralty believes prevention is better than cure – or something like that. We have an interception job to do down south. It's known to the intelligence boys that a Jap naval force and assault landing ships with infantry and gunners are holed up in Last Hope Inlet, which opens off Smyth's Channel. It's believed their intention may be to proceed through the inner channels, keeping clear of Punta Arenas, and enter the Beagle Channel to emerge through the Le Maire Strait into the South Atlantic for the Falklands. They won't come openly around Cape Horn and risk being picked up. They'll wait their moment to come out and head straight for the Falklands from cover.'

'When we engage them? Some hope!' Frome gave a very hollow laugh. 'The Admiral must be off his rocker, sir.'

'Not that far off. Remember that demolition party of sappers, Number One. We go in to block the Japs' passage. If the guesses are correct, there's an especially narrow and shallow passage they'll have to go through. Massive explosions – charges laid to bring down the rock and whatnot and make it unnavigable.'

'Then they slide out the other way, into the Pacific, and risk Cape Horn?'

Cameron shook his head. 'Not quite. Once they know they've been rumbled, it's believed they'll be even less keen to risk Cape Horn. And there's something else: by that time, Admiral Halsey's US South Pacific Command will have had time to rake up a task force to head towards the Magellan Strait and be ready and waiting.' He paused. 'It's all quite neat, really.'

The First Lieutenant blew out his cheeks. 'Well, I'm glad you think so, sir! I'm buggered if I do.'

By the time the corvette had called at Ascension Island and left again on her southward track, the curious processes of the lower deck known as the galley wireless had produced a whole spectrum of rumours, or buzzes, some of which came fairly close to the truth. Not all of them: Able Seaman Fish –

6

Stripey Fish on account of his three good-conduct badges –
had it all wrong as usual but also as usual was listened to in
the messdeck because he had a vivid imagination that helped
to dispel boredom at sea. 'Falklands,' he said. 'Stands to
reason, don't it?'

'What does?' Leading Seaman Hoggett asked, drawing
the back of a hand across his nose. He had a cold coming on ;
the weather was treacherous, getting a bloody sight colder
hourly as they dropped towards the High South Latitudes.
'What's reasonable about the bloody Falklands anyway?'

'Napoleon went there,' Fish said complacently.

'No 'e didn't. That was St Helena.'

'Same thing. We're going to prepare a billet for fucking
'Itler. Never too soon to be ready, like. Put the sod there and
blow 'is balls off with the westerlies.'

'Oh yes,' Hoggett said with a snort. 'Now, I wonder what
give you that lovely idea, Stripey, or did you dream it?'

'Don't get enough sleep to dream. Like I said, it stands to
reason. All dictators end up in the South Atlantic. There's
nowhere to escape to. Worse than bloody Dartmoor.'

'Of which you 'ave personal experience I don't doubt.'

Fish gave a mock swipe in Hoggett's direction. 'Get
stuffed. You see if I'm not right. They're a close lot of sods in
the War Cabinet. Could be Winnie's got 'is hands on 'Itler
already and is going to produce 'im as a surprise to end the
war.'

No one took Stripey Fish seriously at the best of times ; he
gave up and climbed into his hammock for a bit of kip before
going back on watch. A seaman gunner was Stripey Fish by
non-substantive rate ; not a very good one as was well known
to the officers, but if ever he got the chance he would like to
knock off Nazis. But Jimmy the One wouldn't put him on a
gun, not at action stations, and the only thing Fish was likely
to have a chance to knock, and that not before his next leave,
was his old woman back home in Pompey ; she had what he
called a comfortable figure and liked a bit of you-know-what

7

whenever the fancy took him, which was often. She never complained and she liked kids : Stripey had eight. He'd been a bit of a barrack stanchion in his time, so there had been plenty of opportunity although a spell in China had interrupted the continuity and half-way along the line there had been a three-year gap in production. When he'd got back to RNB and wangled himself a nice soft number in the Drafting Office, there had been no holding Em. He'd enjoyed handing out the draft chits that sent other poor daft sods to sea, while staying ashore himself. Stripey Fish knew how to make himself indispensable : work extra hours without moaning – much – except to himself, suck up to the Drafting Master-at-Arms, look smart at all times, be helpful to officers and obey orders promptly and cheerfully. That was the way to stay in barracks. But his luck hadn't held once war had come and he'd been forced to justify his existence as an able seaman by going to sea again. And he detested corvettes with all their discomfort and cramped quarters and the way they seemed to avoid going into port whenever possible. Give him the pusser Navy, the big stuff, battleships, battle-cruisers, aircraft-carriers. He'd done his China-side time in the *Hermes*. It wasn't like being at sea at all. Now the old *Hermes* had gone. The bloody rotten Japs had scored forty bomb hits on her inside ten minutes, not far off Trincomalee.

It was Leading Signalman Black, a Royal Fleet Reservist recalled to the Andrew in 1939, who came closest to the truth when he put his head into the petty officers' mess. 'Falklands,' he said. 'I reckon I know what that means, Chief.' He had addressed Chief Petty Officer Parbutt, the Chief Engine-Room Artificer in charge of the corvette's motive power.

'What ?'

'Defence being strengthened. The Falklands, they're wide open.'

'*We* won't help much.'

'Ah, but maybe more's going in from Simonstown, see. I

8

wouldn't be surprised if them Nazis were casting their eyes at the Falklands, not surprised at all.'

'What would they do with 'em, eh? Place is nothing but piles of sheep shit.'

Leading Signalman Black put a finger to the side of his nose and looked wise. 'Good base. Give 'em a secure presence in the South Atlantic, wouldn't it, so they could attack the convoys coming and going around the bloody Cape. Could have bin made for the purpose.'

'Well, you could be right, but I don't see we're any addition to anyone's defence.' The Chief ERA picked up an ancient copy of the *Daily Mail* and studied a Guinness advert. He could just about do with a Guinness, though it wasn't his usual drink, a shade too heavy for his stomach. He was a plain beer man, always had been ... a bachelor, he spent his leaves with a married sister living in West Auckland in County Durham, passing each evening away with his brother-in-law drinking Sam Smith's. You couldn't beat Sam Smith's and he had a gut to prove how nourishing it was. He began dribbling a little from the corner of his mouth, just at the mere thought of his next leave, Japs permitting if the killick bunting-tosser was right. Bugger the war ... he heaved himself to his feet and went off to his engine-room to take his mind off beer, and off his sister too. His brother-in-law was all right but Vi his sister was a pain in the arse, not being a drinker herself and not being slow to criticize those who were.

Shortly afterwards the leading signalman climbed up to the bridge. Just as he got there the Officer of the Watch, Morgan, sighted something ahead and reported to the Captain. Black scowled; the signalman on watch ought to have seen it first, if not the lookouts, but that Morgan was as sharp-eyed as a ferret.

Cameron brought up his glasses and studied the bearing. 'Ship,' he said. His first command ... and the vessel was hull down, no firm identification possible. 'Action stations,' he

9

said, and pressed the alarm button in front of him. The action alarm sounded raucously throughout the ship and men began to tumble from hammocks, through hatches, out along the upper deck, doubling to their stations. Fifteen minutes later the ship was seen to be what Cameron had in fact believed it might be : RFA *Garsdale*, a little ahead of her ETA and all ready to connect the oil fuel pipelines. There was a good deal of muttering about the new skipper when the word was passed. Edgy bastard, should have realized it would be the oiler. Too bloody keen was Lieutenant-Commander Cameron, one of those RNVRs who were more pusser than the RN itself, out to prove himself. On the bridge Morgan asked permission to secure from action stations.

'No,' Cameron said. 'We remain closed up except for men required to handle the pipeline.'

'But – '

'No buts,' Cameron said crisply. 'Fuelling's when we might be caught with our pants down, Pilot. I'll take the ship now.'

Morgan thought, why not me ? I'm a sight more experienced. But he stood aside from the binnacle and Cameron passed the helm and engine orders to close the oiler and connect up. The operation didn't take very long, even though the lift and scend of the sea didn't help matters. The oiler's crew had had plenty of sea refuelling experience since the outbreak of war, and aboard the corvette the buffer, Petty Officer Lamprey, was a first-class seaman who knew just the right place to use Stripey Fish's overweight to best advantage on hauling in the heavy pipeline.

Fuelling had finished and Cameron had cast off the pipeline and was standing clear of the oiler when something else was sighted, this time by the leading signalman. He yelled it out, no time lost.

'*Green one-six-oh, sir!* Periscope, I reckon.'

Once again Cameron's glasses came up, steadied on the bearing. It was a feather of water, only just distinguishable. The U-boat beneath it . . . its CO would never be expecting

10

to be seen in the prevailing weather conditions of disturbed water, which in any case were not those in which an attack would normally develop. With his ship still ready, closed up at action stations, Cameron grabbed for the tannoy.

'This is the Captain ... submarine at periscope depth on the starboard quarter. I'm going in to attack.'

2

THE inquest on why the Asdic cabinet had failed to report could wait : technical hitches were not unknown.... Cameron, realizing what was about to happen, felt sick to the guts. And a matter of seconds later his fears were proved all too true : the warning signal was still being flashed to the oiler when the torpedo hit. The concussion of the explosion and the searing heat of the fire as the tanks went up swept back over the corvette's exposed decks and bridge. The oiler seemed to vanish, cocooned in a pall of thick, black smoke shot through with red and orange flame. Oil flowed out, burning, covering the surrounding sea with fire. A few men were seen to jump, men who would have fried the moment they hit the flaming oil.

Grim and silent, Cameron stared ahead. Below, the Chief ERA, with his engine giving all it had, watched his dials and gauges, felt the concussion ring through the ship's plating, saw needles jump and flicker and then steady again as the little corvette sped on. Sixteen knots – all she had. Pathetic, Parbutt thought, but with luck just about enough to get to grips with that U-boat, which the skipper had said was not far off. Parbutt prayed that they would get it. There was nothing worse than a tanker going up ; Parbutt had seen it happen before. It had revolted him. The agony of fire ... he shook his mind free of morbid thoughts and waited for the shock of the depth charges.

On the bridge, Cameron, with his Asdics still useless, took

the corvette on towards the submarine's last noted position. By now there was no periscope to disturb the sea's surface; the U-boat, its torpedo discharged, had gone deep, possibly too deep for attack. There was plenty of depth in the South Atlantic; Cameron had ordered the deepest possible setting on the charges, ready in the racks and throwers aft. For the rest he would have to use his judgment and experience and a good deal of sheer guesswork to arrive at the moment when he should give the word to the depth-charge party.

Leading Seaman Plummer was in charge aft. A big unwieldy man whose lantern jaw seemed ever to move in a chewing motion, he held the non-substantive rating of seaman torpedoman and he knew his job. He knew it backwards and he had a sharp eye and a steady nerve. Steady nerve or not, he was shaking with impatience as he awaited the order from the bridge.

'Skipper's cutting it fine,' he said to Petty Officer Gates, PO of the Quarterdeck Division.

'Reckon we're coming over her, do you?'

Plummer nodded heavily. He glanced aft towards the bridge superstructure. 'I heard the perishing Asdic's on the blink. Dunno what experience the skipper's had.'

'You don't get a DSC for nothing, Plum.'

Plummer gave a hoarse laugh. 'Heroics, that's not *experience*, is it?'

Gates was about to say something further when the firing order came down and Plummer lost no time. He roared out, '*Fire!*' The pattern went out, dropped aft from the racks and projected to port and starboard from the throwers. From the bridge Cameron watched the splashes as the charges hit the water.

'Starboard ten,' he ordered.

'Starboard ten, sir.' Morgan, action Officer of the Watch, passed the order down. It was repeated back by the coxswain; the corvette swung, ready if need be to come in for a further attack. Well astern now, the charges detonated and great hummocks of water lifted, spreading, then falling back. Cameron, Morgan and the bridge lookouts watched closely through binoculars.

'No wreckage,' Cameron said. 'I'm going in again. Port five.'

'Port five, sir.'

'Steady!'

'Steady, sir.' Below in the wheelhouse the coxswain brought the helm round to meet and check the swing.

Cameron said, 'Warn the depth-charge party, Morgan.'

'Aye, aye, sir – '

'How's that Asdic?' Cameron swung round to the Asdic cabinet. 'No joy yet?'

'No, sir.' The electrical artificer pushed back his cap, wiped sweat from his forehead. 'Can't isolate the fault yet, sir, but I'll get there.' Bloody thing, the EA thought, it was working right up to the moment it was needed. It wasn't his fault, but he was feeling a personal responsibility all the same. That RFA's crew – poor sods. The Asdic could have saved them if the corvette had got the warning in time and attacked before the U-boat went into action. But what was done . . . the EA shrugged and got on with the job. That was all a bloke could do, that, and try not to think too much about what was going on in that roaring fire and in the sea covered with still-burning oil. Any minute, any day while the war lasted, it could happen to them as well. As he probed and tested, the EA's fingers shook a little and he sweated, not only from the burning oiler's heat. As he worked another pattern of depth charges was dropped and seconds later sent reverberations through the ship. The EA dropped a small screwdriver and cursed aloud. As he scrabbled to retrieve it from the deck of the cramped cabinet he heard a shout from behind him.

'We've got them, Pilot! They're surfacing.' Cameron turned for'ard and leant over the bridge rail to call down to the 4-inch gun's crew. 'Stand by – I'm turning now. Keep the

14

U-boat covered, point of aim the base of the conning-tower, all right ?'

The gunlayer acknowledged. 'Aye, aye, sir !'

A cheer went up as the U-boat was seen to lurch into view, a sinister bow thrusting out from the water, well down by the stern. By now the corvette was turning under maximum wheel ; as Cameron steadied her to give the 4-inch a clear field of fire dead ahead and at the same time present as small a target as he could, the U-boat's conning-tower emerged from the sea and almost at once men were seen to be scrambling from it to man the gun on the casing immediately before the superstructure.

Cameron shouted, 'Open fire !'

The 4-inch crashed out, a harsh, sharp, banging sound that hit hard against the ear-drums. The laying was good, the ranging less so. The shells took the water away beyond the low-set hull of the U-boat. Then the German gunners were in action. A shell screamed low above the corvette's bridge ; instinctively all the personnel ducked as they felt the wind of it. As the heavy surge of the swell threw *Briar* off to starboard, another shell sped over aft, slap above the depth charges. It was lower than the first one : as the projectile screamed away to starboard, Leading Seaman Plummer's body crumpled to the deck, the head taken clean from the neck. Blood spurted horribly, soaking the racks and throwers, spotting the rest of the depth-charge party. Then the corvette's 4-inch found its mark and an explosion was seen at the foot of the conning-tower. Plates fractured ; faces vanished from the conning-tower guardrail and the German gun's crew fell dead or mangled over the casing and into the water. A moment later the bow took a sharper angle and the submarine began to slide slowly back ; she must have been badly damaged in the second depth-charge attack. The conning-tower disappeared below the water.

'Cease firing,' Cameron said. 'Secure depth charges. That's one to chalk up at any rate !'

15

Morgan asked, 'Survivors, sir ?'

'What ?'

'U-boat's crew.' Morgan was looking through his binoculars. 'Bodies in the drink, could be alive.'

Cameron's face was white and set and he felt a shake in his hands. 'We have the oiler's crew to think about first, Pilot. Bugger the Jerries !'

Morgan hadn't liked it. The enemy was the enemy right enough, no disputing that their own side had to come first, but facts had to be faced : there would be no survivors from the oiler. He said as much but Cameron disregarded him and turned the corvette back towards what was left and there wasn't much : the ship had gone and just that spreading carpet of burning oil was left, and in it were corpses, kept afloat no doubt by the heavy oil itself or by the air trapped in their thick clothing which hadn't yet all burned away. As Morgan had expected, there was no one left alive so far as a painstaking search revealed. There was just an appalling stench of oil fuel and charred flesh and when the search was ended Cameron used his binoculars to survey the area where the U-boat had gone down and then, offering no opinion, had passed the order to turn the corvette back on course for the Falkland Islands. Morgan took one look at the Captain's face and bit back what he had been going to say. Most seamen thought the U-boat crews were murderers who deserved no consideration at all ; but there were U-boats and there were submarines – Germans, and British too. No doubt the Nazis thought the same about the British submarines as the British thought about the U-boats. It cut both ways, and more so for Morgan. He had a brother in the submarine service, his elder brother, a lieutenant RN. And he hated to think that something similar could happen to that brother of his. Could even be happening at this very moment. His brother's submarine was operating with the Home Fleet, intercepting blockade runners in the Bay of Biscay, very close to Hitler's France.

16

Nowhere else in the ship was there any criticism of the Captain. The Nasties deserved all they got ; they'd started it in the first place and it had been a U-boat that had sunk the liner *Athenia* right back at the start in thirty-nine – attacked and sunk women and children. Now they'd killed Leading Seaman Plummer as well as the more anonymous crew of the oiler. Why should any of the buggers be picked up ? The skipper was dead right to turn his back on them. The buffer went one further : if a Jerry had been picked up, he'd have stuck his seaman's knife in his gut. Lamprey said as much and his hearers on the quarterdeck, as they cleaned up the mess that had been Leading Seaman Plummer, understood very well indeed. It was common knowledge that the buffer had lost his only son when the old aircraft-carrier *Courageous* – Curry Juice as she had been known to the fleet – was torpedoed off the Bristol Channel, also back in thirty-nine. Blood was thicker than water, after all. And Plummer's was taking a lot of hosing down.

No time was lost in sewing Plummer into his hammock, lead-weighted at the feet. Before the watch was ended Cameron had read the brief committal service and Plummer had slid from beneath the White Ensign, from the tilted plank, to flop formlessly into the South Atlantic. Then the briefly-stopped engines started turning again and the corvette continued on her southerly course. Before the sea committal the First Lieutenant had investigated the failure of the Asdic and had reported to the Captain. No blame attached to anyone in particular. The fact that the set had chosen the very moment of coming action to pack up was just rotten luck.

'Just one of those things,' Frome said with a shrug.

'Perhaps. It's not to happen again, though.'

'No, sir.' Frome turned away and clattered down the bridge ladder, feeling a little on edge. Luck was one of those things, too. You couldn't give orders to luck and expect results. But from this moment on there would be a greater vigilance shown by the EA. In the meantime, the Asdic still wasn't working. Until it was, the whole safety of the ship would lie with the sharp eyes of the lookouts.

Cameron brooded, staring for'ard, shoulders hunched. He was learning the loneliness of command at sea, the loneliness of total responsibility and decision, the loneliness that was brought up cruelly when things went wrong. But slackness in a ship was due to slackness at the top, to the failure of that ship's Captain to set a standard and impose tautness in all departments. That he had only so recently assumed command was no excuse. Command was largely a matter of personality, never of shouting and barking orders. That way simply didn't work ; you had in a sense to permeate a ship with your will ... Cameron gave himself a physical shake as if to clear his mind. He was being over-introspective : mechanical things did have a habit of going wrong at the worst moments, as though they were possessed by some devil of awkwardness. It was just that this one had cost a valuable oiler and a lot of lives.

Eight mornings later the officer of the forenoon watch, Sub-Lieutenant Sykes, raised the northern tip of East Falkland and reported to Cameron from the bridge.

'Captain, sir – Officer of the Watch. Falklands in sight.'

'Thank you. I'll be up.'

Cameron put back the handset of the sound-powered telephone, pushed through the door of his cabin and stepped on to the bridge ladder. Taking up his position by the fore rail he studied the high Falkland hills.

'Bloody world's end,' he said.

'Yes, sir.' Sykes hesitated. 'I wonder what they want us for, sir, what we're going to do there.'

'We'll find out, Sykes.' Nothing had yet gone beyond the First Lieutenant and the navigating officer : the security had been good, though Cameron, aware of the circulating rumours, would be glad enough when the time came to take his whole ship's company into his confidence. He preferred it that way. Men who knew the facts – he'd learned this from Captains he had served under – reacted better. Uncertainty never helped morale or efficiency, but he had his orders and that was that. It would have to wait. From behind, Sykes watched him, then coughed and asked a question.

'Will leave be given, do you think, sir?'

'In the Falklands?' Cameron sounded astonished.

'Yes, sir. I was thinking – '

Cameron turned round. 'Would it be worth having, even if it was given?'

'Well – I don't know. It'd be a change, wouldn't it?'

'A change?' Cameron believed Sykes was making a clumsy attempt to ferret out some information as to what was in store for them. 'We're at war, in case it's escaped your notice,' he added abruptly.

Sykes said in an an aggrieved tone, 'I had just a couple of hours in mind, sir. Stretch our legs. Nothing more than that. Surely we're entitled – '

'You'll have to wait and see,' Cameron said, and turned back to face for'ard again. Sykes scowled; the Captain was an uncommunicative so-and-so, not as *pally* – that was the word – as he would have expected from someone who wore wavy stripes. *Briar*'s last CO had been RNR, nearly as bad as the RN. One would have expected something different from his own cloth of the RNVR; they were all amateurs together, civilians in uniform, in for the duration and not making a career of it. Sykes wished himself, desperately, back in Woolworth's. He'd not been far off getting a manager's job when the war had come along. Woolworth's was a more relaxed atmosphere than the Navy, though of course it was true enough that when you were in management you couldn't be matey with the girls, that would never do, you had to keep your distance and your dignity. Sykes had never even been aware of noticing the charms of some of them; many things passed him by, including the currrent fact that he was known to the lower deck aboard the *Briar* as Weary Willie, also the fact that he had bored his wife stiff before the war and that since he'd been away at sea she'd started an affair with a man beyond call-up age who worked in the Army and Navy Stores and lived in Richmond. Herbert Sykes had been very well satisfied with what he considered a full life: Woolworth's each day except Sundays – he was usually working conscientiously behind the scenes when the staff had their half day, impressing Mr Henry the manager – the odd light ale down the Bricklayer's Arms on Saturday evenings, sometimes with his wife if there was someone to mind the kids, more often alone, after the football match if there was one; the movies every Friday and never mind what was on; the amateur dramatics in which he was quite a lad; and collecting labels off matchboxes. All that, and a patch of garden formed by a square of lawn which he mowed weekly in the summer with a Qualcast and tended a surround of flower beds, and the annual holiday at Bognor Regis when the kids enjoyed the beach and he read Agatha Christie in Penguins.

Pre-war had been very, very good . . . .

The Falkland Islands and what might flow from them held little promise. Meanwhile, as the watch wore on, the Falklands came up more and more bleakly. High peaks and a lot of snow, and a roaring wind that was throwing the *Briar* about like a cork and bringing racing seas to drop aboard amidships and fly in spindrift over the plunging bows. Sykes was already clutching at the binnacle for support; the leading signalman and the port and starboard lookouts didn't seem bothered, but Sykes had never really got his sea-legs and, though no longer sea-sick, never felt well at sea. He wished he'd joined the Army if he had to join something. Or the RAF, with a lovely, comfortable, stationary airfield was probably the best of all. The Brylcreem Boys, and why not?

Briar moved on down the East Falkland coastline, making her approach to Port Stanley. Sub-Lieutenant Morgan was

20

on the bridge by this time, watching bearings and checking with the chart. 'Excuse me,' he said, pushing Sykes away from the binnacle.

'Here, just a minute, will you – '

'I need the azimuth.'

'There's no need to shove.'

'Let go of the bloody binnacle, then. You won't fall over.' Morgan pushed again, harder this time. Sykes scowled but let go and moved away, complaining loudly about manners.

'Sykes,' Cameron said forbearingly.

'Yes, sir? I'd like to – '

'Don't impede the navigating officer.'

'It's all very well – '

'You heard what I said.'

'Yes, but – '

Cameron turned. 'Pipe down, Sykes. That's an order.'

'It's not fair,' Sykes said, not too loudly. Cameron chose not to hear the remark and Sykes muttered inaudibly into the neck of his oilskin.

Two hours later *Briar* was alongside the jetty in Port Stanley harbour. Cameron was saluted over the side by the First Lieutenant soon after a staff car had arrived from the Naval Officer in Charge ; and he was taken to the base to make his report and receive any further orders for his mission. The hands working about the upper deck, making good the depredations of the heavy seas that had been with them for so many days after refuelling, watched the Captain go with much interest and speculation. When he came back, or soon after, they would no doubt learn the worst. None of them doubted that danger lay ahead, and hardship too. A special mission was strongly suspected by now and down here it wasn't like West Africa or the Med – far from it. It was going to be brass monkey weather for God knew how long, Petty Officer Tebbs, the Fo'c'sle Division's PO, said solemnly.

'Keep warm by working 'ard,' he said. 'Starting now, eh, Quinn ?'

Ordinary Seaman Quinn, who had been swinging the lead by leaning on the gun-shield, grinned without rancour. 'Why pick on me, PO ?'

'Not pickin' on you, lad, just saving your mum mourning for you when you freeze to death through bloody lack of motion, that's all.' Tebbs moved on for'ard, seaboots sliding on the wet deck, to take a look at the anchor cable. It had had a bit of a battering, but looked snug enough in the slips and clenches. Tebbs hummed to himself ... *Somewhere in France with you ...* ' Vera Lynn, bless her. But Tebbs' missus wouldn't have her heart in France ; it would be in Freetown or the waters adjacent. She wouldn't know anything about the Falklands, and just as well maybe, since she was the world's worst worrier and would be mightily concerned about nice, thick mufflers and long johns and keeping his feet dried out so as not to catch cold. She was always on about that, suspecting him of a weak chest and too many fags, but who wouldn't have too many at half a crown a hundred, less if you rolled your own from Tickler's tobacco in tiddly green-labelled tins. Half a pound for a bob, fuck a duck, there were plenty of advantages in being recalled to the Andrew. Tebbs missed his wife but had never been happy away from the service and his old mates. Pompey had been home to Tebbs and more than home ; Pompey was a way of life. He hadn't liked moving up into Northamptonshire when he'd gone out on pension, but his wife's old mother was up there, and Maisie had been tearful and he'd given in, the more readily because one of Maisie's uncles had found him a job in Towcester, odd-job man at the Saracen's Head. Not bad at all ; but Tebbs, though not appearing too eager, had been delighted when Neville Chamberlain finally failed in his um-brella-waving peace efforts and had gone to the wireless on 3 September 1939 – a Sunday morning – and said that this country was now at war with Germany. PO Tebbs, Royal Fleet Reservist, had already had his recall papers and when the Southern Railway took him into Portsmouth Town

22

station he felt he had come home. The bluejackets of the Naval patrol in their blanco-ed gaiters, the Petty Officer in charge with his silver whistle and chain ... the sounds of the barracks where new drafts were drilling under the gunners' mates, the hum of activity from all sides, the officers pacing across the parade-ground while junior ratings moved at the double in accordance with routine, the barrack blocks alive with more men than they'd ever been built to accommodate – he was back to life himself.

And the dockyard ...

All the familiar sights and smells, the old boat-yard, tar, oil fuel wafting across from the oil jetties on the Gosport side of the harbour ... the dockyard mateys, working parties of overalled seamen being marched around, Nelson's *Victory* still there in her dry-dock, a battle-cruiser lying at the South Railway Jetty and further along great liners – *Queen of Bermuda*, *Monarch of Bermuda* and others – being stripped of their finery and glitter and transformed into armed merchant cruisers with strengthened decks and 6-inch guns. Tebbs had gone to look at his old home in a road of two-up and two-downs off Arundel Street. It was still there, still looked the same but with a difference: it was no longer a Navy man's home. As he watched nostalgically a man in uniform came out calling goodbye to someone inside, and the uniform was that of the Portsmouth Corporation buses. Tebbs was disappointed. He had local leave till 0800 next day, that first night of his recall, and he spent it partly in the Petty Officers' mess, partly in the Queen Street pubs where he met a number of old shipmates, also on recall from reserve, and got pretty blotto on Brickwood's beer, ending up in Aggie Weston's Royal Sailors' Rest in Commercial Road, a teetotal establishment that didn't mind drunks so long as they didn't drink on Miss Weston's premises and charged only a shilling a night bed-and-breakfast. Good old Aggie, the sailor's friend, always welcoming and good value. No preaching, because Aggie had understood sailors and had left her imprint on her staff accordingly.

Back in the Andrew or not, Tebbs didn't relish the Falklands and he watched Cameron's departure with as much interest and foreboding as the hands working part-of-ship. What a place to fetch up, if that was what was on the cards. About the only sounds, apart from those of the corvette, came from the seagulls. 'Bloody great shite-'awks,' Tebbs said, dodging a bombing run as he had a word with Sub-Lieutenant Thompson who was parading the fo'c'sle with his hands behind his back all neat and pusser and doing his best to look busy just in case he happened to be spotted by the First Lieutenant – a pusser bloke himself, was Jimmy the One. 'Bigger'n those off the west coast o' Scotland, I reckon.'

'They look the same to me,' Thompson said.

Tebbs shook his head. 'Not to me they don't, sir. Shite-'awks vary, you'd be surprised. Little softies down south, get tougher the further north you go. In UK, that is. Off Mallaig, f'rinstance – all those 'errings to attract 'em – they look like bloody murderers with a squawk to match. Maybe it's the weather.' He ran a hand across his jaw. 'Any buzzes, sir?'

'No. We'll hear soon enough, when the Captain gets back.' Thompson welcomed a natter; it made him look occupied, and he kept the conversation going. Trivialities, until he was called aft by Frome, who wanted a word about kit musters, one of the many duties of a divisional officer who was expected to act as nursemaid to his ratings and see that they didn't lose or misuse their gear. Tebbs watched him go, easing his cap from his forehead and giving a wry grin towards the officer's back. The lower deck had it that Mr Thompson had managed a brothel in civvy street – he was all hair oil and smarm but with a watchful look about him, as if, according to Stripey Fish, he expected to be arrested at any moment for living off immoral earnings. In fact it had been Stripey who'd started that particular buzz. Tebbs happened to know that Mr Thompson had been in the Foreign Office

24

and had had the guts to get out and fight the war. You couldn't go by appearances. But maybe, come to think of it, there wasn't all that much difference between the perishing diplomats and the Mother Judge in a brothel . . . they were all a devious lot. Tebbs blew out his frozen cheeks and flapped his arms like a penguin. He looked across the harbour at the residents, as he regarded them since they had that look about them : HMS *Birmingham* and the ex-liner *Asturias*, now an armed merchant cruiser. They were going nowhere, Tebbs reckoned, steam at twenty-four hours' notice and the *Birmingham* with her lower and quarter-booms out and boats lying at them nice and peaceful.

As Tebbs watched a bugle blew stand-easy over the *Birmingham*'s tannoy and what work was in progress on deck ceased instantly as the hands dashed below for a drag and a bar of nutty from the NAAFI canteen. At the same time stand-easy was piped aboard the corvette and similar things happened, though the lads hadn't so far to go to reach their messes. Big ships, Tebbs thought sardonically, all spit and polish and move aside for God the Father, in other words the Captain . . . in his day, pre-war, Tebbs had been a destroyer man and he regarded destroyers as the cream of the Navy. But he was too old for that lark now, or so they'd said at the Pompey drafting office. Old be buggered : corvettes, in fact, were even harder going physically. What they'd meant had been that he was out-of-date and mentally turgid. In the Andrew, you were in your dotage at forty unless you were an admiral. And if that made any kind of sense then Tebbs failed to see it. But one thing was clear : make a balls aboard a corvette and it didn't matter so much as if you made it aboard a destroyer. Corvettes were expendable.

Tebbs was still pondering on expendability when he saw the skipper coming back in the staff car. Piped aboard, Cameron went to his cabin with the First Lieutenant. He was still closeted when an army lorry drove up and stopped alongside and a large party of brown jobs got down and were loudly fallen in by an NCO while an officer and a staff sergeant climbed the gangway to the corvette's quarterdeck. Tebbs stared : sappers. When, within the next half hour – by which time the troops had embarked with a vast amount of explosive material and were cluttering up the decks – Cameron passed the order to clear lower deck and then spoke to the ship's company, Tebbs decided that his thoughts had coincided very nicely with the facts. Expendability was in the air, all right.

3

'WE'RE going to pull it off,' Cameron said. He spoke confidently, trying to assess the reaction of the assembled ship's company. They were pretty phlegmatic, though there had been some pursed lips and *sotto voce* comments after he'd given them the facts. Seamen didn't relish being in enclosed waters; it was a natural response. Cameron went on, 'It's not going to be easy, that's obvious, and speed's going to be vital. The latest intelligence received indicates the Japanese ships are showing signs of readiness to move through from Last Hope Inlet. Once they do move out, they're expected to take around thirty-two hours to reach the narrows where we blow the charges – which have to be set, of course, before their arrival. The flagship's the *Ichikawa*, mounting eight 6-inch guns in twin turrets, plus ack-ack and torpedoes, the usual stuff. It's estimated she won't proceed through at more than say six knots, but she could shorten the time if she decides to take a risk. It's going to take us thirty hours steaming at maximum speed to reach the Le Maire Strait, and another twelve hours, or more depending on what speed we can make once we're inside the Beagle Channel, to reach the point where the sappers lay the charges. So it's going to be a tight-run thing. If any of you have any questions, I'll do my best to answer them. Well? Yes, Cox'n?'

Chief Petty Officer Rodman, torpedo-coxswain, asked, 'Can you say where the intelligence comes from, sir?'

'Agents in Chile, Cox'n. Said to be reliable. We have to

27

take a chance on that, and if after we leave Port Stanley there's any fresh information, a wireless signal will be made to us in Naval cypher. Anything else?'

Cameron looked down on the ship's company from the bridge. A hand went up and a stoker PO asked, what about the *Birmingham* and the *Asturias*?

'They remain on station,' Cameron answered briefly.

There was a general laugh, and a comment about barrack stanchions and the pile-up of tin cans and wardroom gin bottles around the two ships. Cameron grinned back and said, 'They're needed here. Last line of defence for the Falklands themselves. The place is pretty thinly garrisoned.' He had raised this with NOIC; if the Falklands were considered to have any strategic value, surely a full garrison would have been provided rather than leave the islands at the mercy of what was in fact a small enemy force? NOIC had shrugged and looked doleful; the ways of the Admiralty and War Office were often strange and it was likely enough someone had woken too late from a long sleep. A signal had been received indicating that other war theatres had to take priority and the men in the Falklands must do their best to repel any attack with what they'd already got. It was, NOIC said, a crazy way to run a war; and, unknowingly, he had expressed the same view as had Leading Signalman Black aboard the corvette some days earlier: if the enemy took the islands, the WS convoys were going to be put at risk. Back in Freetown Admiral Pegram had in fact made this point; and now Cameron stressed it before dismissing the hands.

'It's a vital job we have to do and I don't want any of you to forget that. If we fail, a lot of our lads coming around the Cape are going to suffer. So keep the end in mind all the way through: safety for the convoys. UK can't keep going without them.' He looked at his watch. 'We leave in three hours, by which time I hope the troops'll have settled down. A stores lighter will be coming alongside in half an hour,' he added, then glanced at the First Lieutenant. 'All right, Number One.'

'Aye, aye, sir.' Frome saluted and passed the order to dismiss. The hands left the fo'c'sle amid a buzz of talk and speculation. One thing was going to be the weather; it was already worsening visibility-wise – the clouds were lying almost on the water and the damp cold seemed to eat right into the bones, defying duffel-coats and oilskins and thick, knitted jerseys, seaboots and heavy, greasy stockings with their tops turned over the boots. The wind, though blowing strongly, had no effect on the visibility, seeming only to blow in more and more cloud to swirl around the corvette. That cloud was as endless as the wind itself: Morgan, on the bridge and busy with his charts, recalled the words of the Admiralty Sailing Directions for the area: the Falklands took two and a half inches of rain a month on average, the sea was never anything less than rough, and the low cloud base could last for days on end. Another hazard when moving through the waters around the islands was kelp, an exceptionally rubbery seaweed that built up huge deposits along the indented coastline and could jam the propellers of ships' boats. To Morgan, accustomed to liners such as *Orion*, *Orama*, *Orontes* and *Otranto*, the little *Briar* was scarcely bigger than a ship's boat and her screw could react to too many dollops of the muck if they were unlucky enough to run into an extensive patch when they approached West Falkland on the return trip and came on to the continental shelf.

Morgan was joined by Sykes. He looked up as the RNVR sub-lieutenant said, 'Last Hope Inlet. Ever been there?'

'My run was to Australia via Suez,' Morgan answered. 'We didn't come this way, buddy! But what's the worry – or is it just the name? If it is, forget it.'

'I don't like the sound of it I must say.'

'I suppose you don't walk under ladders, either.'

Sykes bit his lip; Morgan was very abrasive, no sympathy in him, but he was the navigator and as such would know a thing or two about the pilotage risks in enclosed waters and how they were going to reach their destination. He asked the question direct and Morgan said, 'I'll show you. Look.'

With the tip of a pair of dividers the RNR sub-lieutenant traced a course across the waters leading down towards Cape Horn. He said, 'Once we're through the Le Maire Strait, we head for the Beagle Channel, just as Father said. If you don't know where that is, it's right there – see ?'

Sykes nodded. 'We don't go round Cape Horn, then ?'

'No. Happy now ?'

Sykes disregarded that. 'After the Beagle Channel – '

'We go through into Cook Bay, that's *there* – behind Hoste Island. The Japs'll be coming down from the north and the assumption is that they'll head for the Beagle Channel and out to the open sea. To enter the Beagle Channel they have to negotiate one of two passages round this little islet here.' Morgan put his dividers on a small island, roughly triangular in shape, standing in Cook Bay at the entry to a narrow strip of water leading into the Beagle Channel proper. 'They could choose either way – they're both very dicey, both surrounded by high rock faces, but it's believed they'll choose the northern passage because there's a shade more water beneath them. That happens to suit our particular purpose, because to get into the north channel they have to enter what's in fact – for a short distance – the narrowest part in the whole bloody maze. Right there, in fact.'

Morgan indicated a protruding thrust of land on the island's north-western tip. The channel between this and the mainland of Tierra del Fuego was certainly narrow, and, according to the chart, there were shoals that narrowed it still further. 'Just about room enough for them,' Morgan said. 'But once we get there, there won't be, not any longer.'

'How's it going to be done ?' Sykes asked, sounding anxious.

Morgan rolled up his chart and stared back at the RNVR

30

sub-lieutenant. 'You've picked my brains navigationally,' he said. 'My brief ends there. When Father's ready to tell you more, no doubt he'll do so.'

Sykes flushed ; he was well aware that Morgan had no time for him at all, that he regarded him as of no account in the ship. It was unpleasant to know that Morgan wasn't alone in this. CPO Rodman, the coxswain, was politely forbearing with him, so was the buffer . . . Sykes really couldn't understand why. Surely it was natural enough for him to make no bones about the fact that he much preferred, say, Richmond Hill to the bloody South Atlantic ? *He* hadn't wanted to go to war and it would be plain daft to make any pretence that he had. Rotten little boat, he detested every minute of the time he spent aboard it. It was a life of overcrowded horror, and now, with the sappers aboard, it was going to be more claustrophobic than ever. The wardroom was little bigger than a cupboard and one Army officer would make all the difference . . . not that it was so important when set against the other considerations, those of life and death. Sykes gave a sudden shiver as he went down the bridge ladder: Last Hope Inlet !

Stores were taken when the lighter came alongside : mostly tinned stuff, bully beef, condensed milk, plus some potatoes in sacks. More ammunition as well, including replacement depth charges for what use they were likely to be behind Cape Horn. When stores had been taken the *Briar* shifted alongside an oiler and once again topped up her fuel tanks, after which the hands were piped to stations for leaving harbour. They fell in fore and aft, duffel-coated and seabooted, stood to attention when the Captain piped a salute to NOIC as they moved past the Naval base, then fell out to make a close stow of all deck gear in preparation for bad weather. Gales, not unexpectedly, were predicted for the Cape Horn area ; and as they came out from the bleak dreariness of Port Stanley they began to meet the roaring westerlies, just the

31

edge of them so far, and the bucketing began. Their future looked as bleak as the Falklands themselves. Cameron remained on the bridge, tending his ship through the bad weather; he would be there most of the way through, at least until he fell asleep on his feet. In the past he had held critical thoughts of Captains who in his view overdid the bridge-keeping, often to the point where they would be too tired to function with a clear brain in an emergency. Now, he was beginning to understand. Everything aboard was the Captain's final and inescapable responsibility and there were times, such as now, when the Captain had to be around to take it, to make instant decisions and hope to God they were the right ones.

Already the trouble had started in a minor way. Sykes, unseamanlike as ever, had got in the way of a sling from the stores lighter and something heavy had landed on his right foot. Sykes had made a great hoo-ha about terrible pain and Cameron had felt bound to make a signal to NOIC requesting medical attention. A surgeon lieutenant had been sent across from the *Asturias* and had listened to a tale of woe; but had pronounced Sykes not bad enough to be landed. The bruise, which basically was all it was, would heal in a day or so. In the meantime he bandaged it and gave Sykes a sedative, recommending to Cameron that the injured officer be put off duty for the rest of that day and turned to again thereafter. The lower deck's opinion, not too softly expressed, was that Mr Sykes was suffering a self-inflicted wound and it had failed to come off. Cameron was inclined to agree; Sykes was just the sort to try to slide out from under if he could. The lower deck went even further with its comments: if something had to land on Sykes, it was a flaming pity it hadn't landed somewhere more useful, like his head. Anyway, the upshot of it all was that young Carruthers, the RNVR snotty, was taking a watch on his own, something he hadn't done before. That was another reason why Cameron had decided to remain on the bridge after moving clear of pilotage waters

32

to head south-west for the world's storm-tossed end.

He glanced over his shoulder. Carruthers was standing rigid at the binnacle, holding tight and looking scared stiff at his responsibilities.

'All right, Mid?'

'Yes, thank you, sir.'

'Try to look it, then.'

'I'm sorry, sir.'

'The ship won't bite.'

'Oh no, sir!'

Cameron stifled a sigh and moved back to stand alongside the midshipman. 'All you have to do is remain alert, chivvy the lookouts if they're *not*, and watch the course. Who's on the wheel?'

'I'm afraid I don't know, sir.'

Cameron said, 'Then find out bloody fast! You should always know that.'

'Yes, sir.' What was visible of Carruthers' face behind the balaclava and the hood of his duffel-coat was deeply flushed; at any rate, Cameron thought, his blood hadn't frozen yet. The midshipman bent to the voice-pipe, sounding apologetic. 'I'd like to know the name of the helmsman, please.'

'Aye, aye, sir. Fish, sir, able seaman.'

'Right. Thank you, Fish.'

Down below, Stripey Fish gave an unkind grin. He knew the score, knew that Carruthers was being hazed by the skipper for what he'd left undone. Putting on a concerned voice Stripey spoke back up the voice-pipe. 'Anything else you wants to know, sir?'

'Er – no thanks, Fish. Nothing.'

'Sure, are you, sir? Anything to oblige – '

'No, thank you. It's quite all right, Fish.'

'It'd be no trouble to – '

Cameron put his mouth down to the voice-pipe. 'Pipe down, Fish.'

'Sorry I'm sure, sir.' Fish winked across at the quarter-master, Leading Seaman Hoggett. Shielding the end of the voice-pipe with his hand, he murmured, 'Silly young sod, still in 'is nappies I shouldn't wonder. 'E's too *perlite* to be a proper officer.'

'We was all young once,' Hoggett said, sniffing. His perishing cold was no better. He closed one nostril with his thumb and blew down to the wheelhouse deck through the open one.

'Not me,' Stripey said, keeping half an eye on the gyro repeater. 'Time I was 'is age, I done me time at Shotley and got licked into shape. I'd 'ad me first tart when I was sixteen, and I bet that middy 'asn't 'ad one yet.'

Stripey's hand wasn't a very efficient tamping device and his voice had risen a little, so that Carruthers got the unintended message and flushed again, more deeply this time. Stripey had hit a raw spot ; Carruthers had never managed to summon up the courage. The circles in which his wealthy parents moved were ones circumscribed by upbringing and because he'd lived at home young ladies who had been taught proper behaviour rather than contraception were young Carruthers' only female contacts. They knew that sex did not take place in Pinner and Northwood. Inhibited was a gross under-statement ; they belonged to the school that thought sex dirty and unnecessary other than in the line of duty. Young Carruthers had never even attempted to break through the mould, much though he would have liked so to do. He feared horrified rejection and he feared a report to his parents who, though indulgent with money, shared wholeheartedly the mores of their suburb. Life as a result had been rather dull : formal parties, theatres, a little boating on the river, holidays in Scotland, tennis, that sort of thing. There had been talk of sending young Carruthers to Cambridge, but it hadn't got beyond talk since young Carruthers was known not to have the application to take exams. In a way, the war had come as something of a release. But nothing had yet broken down the long implanted inhibitions and Carruthers was a virgin. He'd been one so long that he felt he would never recognize the moment when it came, the moment when it would be acceptable and safe to make a proposition, say to a Wren. He was aware that Wrens, the commissioned ones in particular, were known throughout the Navy as officers' mattresses but if this was true then *he*'d never settled down on one.

And now he was scared, and very sorry indeed for himself as well. This mission sounded extremely dangerous and Carruthers believed they weren't going to come back from it. So much could go wrong and they seemed in any case to be relying on guesswork; and it would be cruel, really dreadful, if he should die before he'd had a ... well, that was a crude, lower-deck way of expressing it, but before he'd had what, if you believed their stories, every other man had ten times a day on leave, lucky so-and-sos. *He* hadn't even got a girlfriend; only mother and father awaited news of him in Pinner.

'Watch it!' Cameron said without turning.

'Sir?'

'Ship's head, Mid. It's paying off. Give that fat helmsman a rocket.'

'Oh, yes, sir.' Once again Carruthers bent to the voice-pipe to deliver his rocket to a man who seemed to sense his past frustrations. 'I say, Fish. Do watch your course, will you? You're a little off. The – the Captain's noticed it.'

'Oh, I say, sir,' Fish said up the pipe, grinning. 'Didn't notice it yourself, I s'pose, sir?'

'No,' Carruthers answered before he'd thought it out properly. Anger came to him. 'Don't be bloody impertinent,' he snapped, and flushed again.

'That's better,' Cameron said. In the wheelhouse, Stripey ruminated, chewing like a cow on a piece of spearmint. The middy was learning after all; give him another few months and he'd be as bloody rude as the Captain of a battlewagon. If they lived that long.

35

Briar's mission had been originated, and her current movements were being so far as possible monitored, in the operations room deep down in the concrete excrescence built on to the Admiralty on a corner of Horse Guards Parade. *Briar* was a small ship, quite unimportant in herself. But what she had to achieve was big enough if the convoys were to pass in safety to and from Simonstown and the Indian Ocean. At the time Carruthers and Stripey Fish were exchanging words, the Duty Captain in the ops room was conferring with a rear-admiral.

'Diversions,' he said. 'That's what we need.'

The Rear-Admiral raised his eyebrows. 'In regard to this corvette, what's her name – '

'*Briar*, sir.'

'Ah yes, *Briar* . . . RNVR chap in command?'

The Duty Captain nodded. 'Cameron. Has a DSC.'

'Ah, yes, good show. Right man in the right place and all that – we need a touch of unorthodoxy at times, you know. RNVR's that if nothing else, what?' The Rear-Admiral gave a plummy laugh; he was a plummy man, purple faced and with a large stomach, with grey-white bushes of hair on his cheekbones, what was known as Admiral's Fluff. He was also rigidly orthodox though he didn't think of himself as such and he tended to patronize the reserves, both of them. 'But about this diversion, Bassett. Is it necessary?'

'I think we have to lull the Japanese, sir.'

'Into believing they've not been rumbled d'you mean?'

'Yes. And something else. Something opposite but not necessarily opposed, if you follow.'

'No, I don't.' The Rear-Admiral looked puzzled. He lit a cigarette and inhaled, then blew the smoke out again in a brownish cloud. The initial virgin blue had vanished into his lung structure. 'Be more precise, Bassett.'

'I think,' Captain Bassett said carefully, 'that it would do no harm if the Japanese were made to think we have more strength in the area – '

36

'Around the Falklands?' the Rear-Admiral interrupted keenly.

'Yes, sir. More than in fact we've got. It might make them pause – just might.'

'In case *Briar* fails, d'you mean?'

'Yes.'

'Oh, we mustn't consider *failure*, Bassett!' The Rear-Admiral looked scandalized. 'She's not going to fail – Winston's very expressive about this operation, you know. *Very* expressive, he's been on the phone several times – I expect you know that, actually.'

'Yes, I do, sir.'

'Well, then, you'll get my point. No failure. It's all a damn nuisance, coming now when we're fully stretched over half the blasted world, but there it is, we *must* consider the convoys. Falklands themselves ... God!' The Rear-Admiral came close to echoing the words of Chief ERA Parbutt aboard the corvette. 'Dung and tallow. Damn-all else.'

'Tallow, sir?'

'They export it – I read about it somewhere. What a life. However, let me have your views on diversions and whatever else it was you said.'

'Yes, sir. It's quite simple really. Falklands. 1914 – Battle of the Falkland Islands. Sir Doveton Sturdee – '

'I served under Sturdee as a snotty. Grand chap – so was poor Cradock. Awful pity about Coronel – damned Admiralty simply wouldn't reinforce Cradock's squadron !'

'Yes, sir. What I – '

'There's a memorial to him in York Minster, did you know? I always make a point of paying my respects whenever I'm up that way. However, go on.'

Bassett was showing impatience. He said, 'In regard to my suggestion of making the Japanese fleet believe we have more ships down by the Falklands ... I think we could do that by some carefully worded signals addressed to mythical ships – '

'Mythical ships said to be off the Falklands, Bassett? Yes, could be a good idea, that. But where does the 1914 show come in?'

Bassett smiled. 'Just a bit of bull, sir. England's glorious past. A phantom squadron, proceeding south-west from Freetown as reinforcements and already well on their way. We make signals using the call-signs of the *Invincible* and the *Inflexible*.'

'The ships that beat the buggers back in fourteen ... yes, I like that!' The Rear-Admiral swung himself from side to side in his swivel chair, eyes bright. 'Damn good – but won't the Japs tick over, Bassett?'

'I doubt it, sir. The out-dated call-signs won't convey anything to them, the actual ship names won't in fact emerge. As I said, it's just a bit of – of jingoism, I suppose you could call it.'

'Yes, I see. It appeals, Bassett, it appeals – I was in the old *Invincible* myself, of course – '

Bassett interrupted, 'It also has the merit that no *real* ship – no ship still afloat, I mean – will read and act accordingly.'

'Quite. Well, I see no harm in it.'

'Then may I go ahead, sir?'

'Yes. I'll authorize it – no need to refer it elsewhere, I think.' The Rear-Admiral noted the time as he reflected on certain of his wife's shopping requirements. 'Flag Officer West Africa to make a number of signals to *Invincible* and *Inflexible*, containing cogent orders since we can take it the Japanese will be able to decypher them – excellent!' He knew that at this particular date of the month the Naval recoding and recyphering tables were due to make the routine change, and it was always assumed that towards the end of each period the enemy would have cracked them. 'Tell Pegram he's to arrange a communications balls-up – the out-of-date tables are to be used after the change-over, to make sure those yellow buggers read the signals. D'you know, I think both poor Cradock and Sturdee would have enjoyed this!' He heaved himself to his feet. 'Better see to it right away. Matter of urgency – top priority.' He glanced at a clock on the bulkhead. 'I'll have to be off, Bassett – hold the fort, all right? My wife's got a dinner-party this evening and I promised to do some damn shopping . . . .'

If the ship's company of *Briar* had been able to eavesdrop on the Admiralty they would have been far from surprised at a certain cavalier attitude towards their future. Authority had never bothered very much about the corvettes, even though men died when they went down just as men died aboard the more glamorous ships of the Navy. Families were left shattered to the same degree – but the big ships were prestige ships and when one of them went, like the *Hood*, the *Royal Oak*, *Repulse* and *Prince of Wales* it was a national disaster. Dinner parties would be forgotten and admirals' wives left high and dry.

Quinn, ordinary seaman, aged twenty and not long in the Andrew, felt all this just as much as the seasoned hands and the old guard of the Fleet Reserve. He had been born and bred in Portsmouth and the Navy was in a sense woven into the fabric of his life although the family had no Naval connections at all – his father worked in Pink's the grocers in Palmerston Road in Southsea, or had until the Nazis had flattened the whole area with their air raids in 1941. Everything had gone that night and Palmerston Road had been left a smoking, burning wilderness. After that his father had moved to Chichester and got a job with French's the wholesale grocers. But Pompey was still home to Ordinary Seaman Quinn and he had vivid memories of the great ships that used to move in and out past the Round Tower, between there and the long grey walls of Fort Blockhouse, home of the submarine service. Whenever he could he used to go down and watch, see the ships' companies fallen in from stem to stern, the gun turrets trained to the fore-and-aft line, the Royal Marine bands playing as they moved out for foreign service, or the long paying-off pennant floating from the main when they came back from a commission in the Mediterranean or China.

It had been a kind of glory in its own right, and it had been that sort of thing Quinn had joined for. Plenty of hostilities-only ratings were glad enough to be in the corvettes and miss out on the big-ship bullshit, but not Quinn. He wanted to listen to the bugles and the bands, to be part of a stately entry into Gibraltar or Malta harbours, with an admiral's flag above him and straight stripes galore, with chief gunner's mates, and chief torpedo-gunner's mates and chief yeomen of signals all looking smart and efficient and properly shaved. Aboard the corvettes hardly anyone bothered to shave at sea, never changed their underwear, didn't even wash much. Stripey Fish ran a sort of competition with himself to see how long he could wear a pair of socks ; his record to date was two months day and night. In all that time he hadn't washed his feet.

To Quinn, it wasn't the Navy.

On the night following the discussion of *Briar*'s movements thousands of miles to the north, Quinn, off watch, was putting his point of view to his friend Ordinary Seaman Beaner. Beaner didn't agree ; he liked the free-and-easy ways of the corvettes.

'Stuck-up sods in the big stuff,' he said. 'Don't even know they're born. Never get their feet wet.'

'Bollocks. Know what they used to say about the *Repulse*? Biggest submarine afloat. Used to ship water along the messdecks whenever there was a sea running.'

'That's not what I meant. They don't face hardship – that is, not till they got sunk.' Beaner added quickly, seeing sudden anger in Quinn's face and in any case not wanting to decry men who'd given their lives. He was willing to admit that when the big stuff got it, it was probably a sight worse than being aboard a small ship where you hadn't got far to go to jump overboard. All that maze of ladders and alleyways,

40

all twisted up into knots when a projy came through . . . no, that wasn't good at all and they could keep it. Beaner yawned ; basically, the Navy bored him and he didn't want to talk about it. He was concerned with his own future movements and the prospect of coming to grief somewhere in the days ahead and that was just as far as his interest went. Off watch all he wanted to do was to get his head down in his hammock and dream of home and a girl called Alice who worked in the Home and Colonial Stores in his home town, a real smart girl that his mum said was tarty. His mum couldn't stand her at any price, being infuriated at the way Alice tossed her head at her whenever she said something that Alice didn't agree with, which was roughly one utterance in three. The result of this was that often enough the dreams turned into nightmares in which mum was strangling Alice with her big hands all red from doing the washing, and when the strangling was over Alice's head was tossing all by itself, detached from her body. Beaner, having broken off the conversation with Quinn and got into his hammock, was having this recurrent nightmare when the alarm rattlers sounded stridently, the nearer one almost in his ear.

4

THE visibility was appalling now; it had worsened as soon as *Briar* had cleared away from the Falklands. The cloud base was right down on the water and the wind was murder, gusting beyond Force 12 on the Beaufort Scale. Spray came almost solid over the bows, soaking through the outer clothing of the 4-inch gun's crew, flinging over the exposed bridge to bring an equal wetness to the men on watch. Cameron, at the fore rail, took the brunt of it almost without feeling it. The whole world was a blanket of wetness and discomfort and everything in the ship was straining, creaking and groaning as though attempting to beat the racket of the wind that howled ceaselessly, battering the mast and funnel. Cameron, knowing the urgency of his mission, was taking a risk and keeping the speed up. He thought it unlikely that any shipping would lie in his path – NOIC at Port Stanley had said that there were no other British ships in the area and no reports had been received from the intelligence services that any enemy ships were around either. So the way should be clear. Should be but wasn't . . .

He had just sent down to ask the sapper major to join him on the bridge for a discussion of the *modus operandi* once they were inside the Beagle Channel when the radar reported an echo dead ahead eight miles. This couldn't be land by any stretch of the imagination.

Cameron said, 'Action stations,' and reached down for the

button. Along with Ordinary Seaman Beaner, the hands off watch tumbled from their hammocks and began a controlled stampede to get on deck or below to the engine-room and damage control positions. The ship had closed up and Morgan had taken over the watch from the midshipman within ninety seconds.

'What's it about, sir?' he asked.

'Radar report, Pilot. Echo dead ahead eight miles, closing. Something sizeable.'

'We haven't anything on the plot,' Morgan said.

'Bugger the plot, this is fact, not fiction.'

Behind Cameron, Morgan grinned. Often enough, the plot did turn out to be fiction, but even so he was very surprised that any ship should manifest down here. It was many, many years since the old Cape Horn route had been used except by a handful of refrigerated meat ships, and since the outbreak of war even the neutrals had preferred to join the convoy system, which certainly didn't operate around the Horn. Morgan asked, 'Just a single echo, sir?'

'Yes. Could be anything.'

'What do you mean to do?'

'See if he alters – assuming he has radar himself, he'll have picked us up too.'

'You won't alter yourself, sir?'

Cameron said, 'Not yet anyway. I want to see his reaction first.'

'We won't see a thing in this soup,' Morgan said. 'Never mind the fact that it's dark too – '

'You know what I mean, Pilot.'

Morgan blew out a long breath. He believed the Captain was taking an undue risk in maintaining his course. *When both side lights you see ahead, starboard helm and show your red*, that was what the regulations said. Never mind that right now you couldn't see – the radar was seeing for you and telling you, and what it was saying, since the echo was closing, was that the unknown vessel was coming straight for them on a reciprocal of their own course. Morgan, trained to Merchant Service concepts of ship safety, reacted instinctively against any threat of a collision.

He said, 'It's my job to offer advice, sir.'

Cameron nodded. 'Sure. And I'm here to consider it, so go ahead.'

'I'd alter a little to starboard, sir. Just to be on the safe side. I don't see that we'd lose anything.'

'I'm leaving it to the last moment, Pilot. It's so bloody thick . . . if we're really close I may see what she is. It may be necessary to make a report to NOIC.'

'Break wireless silence?'

'I don't know yet. If she's a German or Jap warship, the Falklands must be warned whatever the risk to ourselves.'

Morgan nodded; he could appreciate Cameron's point all right. *Briar* was not of much account, and her whole mission was to protect the Falkland Islands. If the Japs were already on track for the Falklands, her original mission was already out-dated and the warning would indeed be vital. In any case, he'd had his say and now it was, as ever, all in the Captain's lap. Meanwhile the ships were closing at an estimated combined speed of some thirty-two knots. In fifteen minutes the crunch would come. And if Cameron didn't alter in time, it would be a very wet one.

Amidships at the searchlight platform, two members of the ship's company had taken up their action stations, the old and fat and the young and slim – Stripey Fish and Midshipman Carruthers. Both were aware that they had been allocated the searchlight because it wasn't a demanding job. Stripey Fish knew he was considered too unhandy to do much else in action; and Carruthers knew that the Captain and First Lieutenant doubted his capacity to make fast decisions in any action position that really counted. Here, he had simply to take orders from the bridge and when necessary see to it that Able-Seaman Fish pointed the searchlight in the required direction.

For a start, he decided to assert his authority and he did so by giving an unnecessary order.

He said, 'Keep close to the lever, Fish. We may be wanted at split-second notice.'

'Think so, do you, sir?'

'Yes.'

'Never bin wanted yet, we 'aven't. An' a fat lot o' good the searchlight'd be in this perishin' muck.'

'Never mind that, Fish, just do as I say.'

Stripey Fish muttered to himself, inaudibly. Carruthers was busy remembering what he'd overheard about him never having had a woman. That rankled, and it affected his temper now and made him spiteful. He said sharply, 'Don't drip or I'll put you in the report for dumb insolence, Fish.'

'Oh, yes, sir? You an' 'oo else, might I enquire? Dumb insolence my arse, beggin' your pardon like.' Fish gave a smirk. 'Dumb insolence was bloody dropped from the Articles of War bloody years ago! 'Snot a charge any more, see.'

Carruthers went red. To cover it he pulled down the hood of his duffel-coat and turned his back on Fish. The man was an abomination. . . . Carruthers shrank back into the frugal cover provided by the canvas dodger around the searchlight platform, thinking murderous thoughts. Then he was over-come by a series of yawns, gaping ones. God, he was tired, really shagged out. Action stations had drawn him from a hammock provided from the effects of Leading Seaman Plummer – his bunk in his shared cabin having been turned over to the sapper major – and really he was only half awake. He squatted on his haunches, bringing his whole body into the lee of the dodger, and the wind fell away from him. That was more comfortable. But squatting was not comfortable at all after a couple of minutes and he slumped to the deck, feet outstretched, back against the guardrail-supported dodger.

More yawns and Carruthers began to nod off. Stripey Fish looked down at him sardonically. Daft little sod, going to sleep at action stations. Some example! At the same time Fish had some sympathy: he knew just how easy it was to do. One minute you were awake, the next you'd gone to sleep. It was even possible, if you were tired enough, to do it on the move. But it was asking for trouble and not to be recommended. Fish turned as he heard someone approaching along the deck below.

The buffer, PO Lamprey, checking round the upper deck.

'Well, Fish. All correct? Where's the officer, eh?' The buffer climbed up to the searchlight platform.

'Gone to beddy-byes,' Fish said sententiously.

'Wake 'im up, then, do 'im a good turn.'

'Why?'

''Cos I said so, that's why. Jimmy's not far behind.' Lamprey went on his way, going aft. A moment later, the First Lieutenant loomed and Stripey Fish bent down to the sleeping midshipman.

He gave him a hard shake. 'Wake up, sir,' he said in a hiss.

Carruthers woke. 'You're not supposed to touch an officer when waking him,' he said sourly.

'Officers aren't s'posed to be asleep at action stations,' Stripey said, 'so sod that for a lark, young sir. First Lootenant's coming.'

Carruthers scrambled to his feet, no time lost. He was looking alert enough by the time Frome hailed the searchlight platform.

'All right, Mid?'

'Yes, sir. Any information yet?'

'Nothing so far. We just wait and see what the contact is.' The First Lieutenant went on aft, following the buffer's track. He knew perfectly well that Lamprey had already done all that was necessary and that if there had been anything needing his attention he would have been informed, but the bullshit held as ever. If anything did go wrong,

46

inquests would be the order of the day and he as the responsible officer would carry the can for not having checked round personally. And Lieutenant Frome was RN ; as such he had no intention of putting himself in a position where he might be bawled out by the RNVR. It was a curious situation in any case, the amateur taking command of the professional. A lot of RN officers would have been quietly mutinous about that. It seemed to work in the Army, but the Navy was a different kettle of fish and guarded its professionalism very jealously indeed, and a pretty large proportion of RN officers were cast in a very rigid mould of total superiority and arrogance. They'd been trained for that, all of them – except the special entry ones who joined at seventeen and a half – from the age of a little over thirteen. The Royal Naval College at Dartmouth turned out a very moulded product. Frome himself had gone through it but it had failed to dehumanize him or to alter his outlook on those aspects of the service that he grouped under the general heading of bull. One of the things that he put into this category was the obligation to salute the quarterdeck every time you came aboard and every time you stepped on to it from the after screen – just because, back in almost prehistoric times long before Nelson, the Host was carried on the quarterdeck. The Host, Frome understood, had something to do with the crucifixion and no doubt it had been fair enough to salute it when it was present, but it hadn't been for one hell of a long time now.

Frome reached the depth charges, had a word with the leading seaman who had taken over after Plummer's death, then turned to go for'ard again and report to the Captain. He thought once more about the RNVR. Cameron was all right and had his, Frome's, respect. He knew his job and had proved a good ship-handler, and his record, which had preceded him out to Freetown, could hardly be bettered. Time on the lower deck of a destroyer, during which he'd been personally responsible for despatching a U-boat in the North Atlantic by chucking a grenade down the conning-tower hatch when the Nazis had tried to board, some good work in the Greek islands after being commissioned as a sub-lieutenant, hectic days in north Norway, on Arctic convoys, in the Med where he'd been present at the North African landings . . . and that DSC. A good chap; but Frome still wasn't going to risk rebukes. Perhaps that was a good thing: it kept him on his toes. And the war wouldn't last for ever.

He reported to the bridge. As he got there a voice-pipe whistled and Cameron bent to answer it.

'Captain here.'

'W/T office, sir. We've picked up a signal addressed to a call-sign we can't identify but we believe it's British, sir.'

'Who's the originator?'

'Flag Officer West Africa, sir.'

'Corrupt group?'

'No, sir. Came through as clear as a bell.'

'If you get any more, take 'em down in full,' Cameron said, and banged back the cover of the voice-pipe. He found his fingers were shaking. Continual reports were coming through from the radar; the ship ahead was not far off now and holding its course and speed. It had to be someone unequipped with radar – unless its Captain was doing the same thing as himself, intending to find out his identity and cutting it fine, again like himself. Cameron glanced aside at his First Lieutenant. 'What d'you think, Number One?'

'I think we'll have to alter, sir.'

Cameron nodded but said nothing further. His hands gripped the guardrail tightly. Blood drummed in his ears. He felt that it was vital to try to get a sighting through the murk, vital to be in a position to report any enemy movements. Now the radar was indicating no more than eight cables'-lengths between the ships. He wouldn't be justified in hazarding his ship further. Without turning he called, 'Starboard five.'

A breath of relief came from Morgan as he passed the order down. The coxswain's voice came back hollowly: 'Starboard five, sir. Five of starboard wheel on, sir.'

'Steady,' Cameron said.

'Steady,' Morgan repeated.

'Steady, sir. Course, 227, sir.'

Cameron nodded. Down the voice-pipe Morgan said, 'Steer 227.'

Now the radar bearing was altering. Cameron found his body wet with sweat as the unknown ship was brought across to port to come close down his side. 'All of you watch out to port,' he snapped. His own glasses were already trained on the bearing. They all saw it together: Cameron, Frome, Morgan, Leading Signalman Black and the port bridge lookout. But they saw nothing more than a shape – nothing more, really, than a darker patch in the filthy night. Nothing identifiable. It was just a moving object.

Cameron swore. 'Any of you see any more than I did, which was damn little ?'

They had not. Frome said, 'Could have been a warship, sir, could have been a merchantman.'

'And any nationality you care to name.'

'Yes, sir. And dead silent . . . no engine sounds, yet she was bloody close.' Frome gave a somewhat nervy laugh. 'That legend, the one about the *Flying Dutchman*. That was somewhere around here, wasn't it ? A bloody ghost ship . . .'

Cameron laughed. 'No. Off the Cape of Good Hope, Number One. Captain van Straaten, condemned to spend his life beating up against the westerlies till Doomsday, and never make the port of heaven. But we're not in the business of seeing ghosts, Number One – nor is the radar !'

When the reports indicated the contact drawing well astern, Cameron passed the order to secure from action stations.

Below in the small mess allocated to the communications ratings, Leading Signalman Black was nattering to his oppo, Leading Telegraphist Jock Frazer, who came from Inverary in Argyll ; Frazer was still being nagged at by the unidentifiable call-sign. Probably the matter was unimportant; his first thought had been that the transmitting W/T operator in Freetown had made a balls and got the call-sign wrong. But that had failed to wash. For one thing naval telegraphists were always pretty hot and could well assess the weight of gilded wrath that would drop from on high to obliterate anyone who made a balls of such a basic thing as a call-sign. And then, finally to dispose of the balls-up theory, another transmission had been picked up addressed to the same call-sign as the first one. This had been passed to the coding officer for decyphering and Frazer didn't know what was in it. Cyphers were not for ratings.

'Bloody mystery,' he said to Black, 'why anyone should make to a ship that don't exist, it has me beat.'

Black nodded and rolled himself a fag. Lighting the somewhat straggly result, he asked without too much interest, 'What was the call-sign, eh?'

Frazer told him.

'Eh?' Black stared.

Frazer repeated it.

'Well, stone my Aunt Fanny's bum,' Leading Signalman Black said in amazement.

'What's up, then?'

'You don't bloody recognize that call-sign?'

'I said I didn't.'

Black nodded, an introspective look in his eye as he went back into the past. He said, 'No, before your time, mate. My first ship ... I was a signal boy in 'er ... the old *Inflexible*. Battle-cruiser under Sir Doveton Sturdee.'

'Battle o' the Falkland Islands ...'

Black nodded. 'Dead right! I wasn't with 'er then, got landed sick just before the squadron left UK. My first ship, see – 'er pennants *and* 'er wireless call-sign, Christ, they're engraved on me 'eart like that there Joan of Arc, 'oo 'ad Calais on 'ers if I remember right.'

Frazer gave him a hard look. 'Sure of this, are you, dead sure?'

'Just said so. *Course* I am!'

Frazer got to his feet. 'Better let the skipper know,' he said. Then he paused, frowning and running a hand across a jaw dark with lack of recent shaving. 'It's a funny thing,' he said.

Black looked up. 'What is? I can't see – '

'A signal to a ship that was in action around here back in fourteen . . . and some unknown ship passing us just a wee while back – and at about the same time as that first signal was sent, what's more. You said Jimmy was nattering about the *Flying Dutchman.*' Frazer left the messdeck after giving what Black thought was a faintly sinister laugh. Black dragged at his cigarette and stirred uneasily on the locker he was using as a seat. Jock Frazer was a Highlander, all – what was the word – fey and gloomy. Scots, especially Highlanders, tended towards a degree of weirdness. They saw things that other people didn't, or anyway they made out they did, some of them. Could be the whisky, but not at sea. Once, and that time it *had* been the whisky, when *Briar* had been based at Greenock, Leading Telegraphist Frazer had seen Bonnie Prince Charlie coming up the Clyde, past the boom that stretched across from Cloch Point, in what he said was a coracle, waving a claymore and swearing furiously about the English. Frazer had even heard the pipes, clear over the water. He'd got a bit violent about it, wanting to join the prince, and Black had had the devil's own job getting him back aboard without incurring police interest.

Black gave a sudden shiver of apprehension. The *Flying Dutchman* had always been a symbol of bad luck. He told himself not to be bloody daft, all that was just fantasy and never to be taken seriously. It wouldn't have been, not in Pompey, or Guz, or even rotten old Freetown come to that. Down here it was different. And, even though it was around twenty-eight years since the old *Inflexible* had steamed south for the Falklands, and had long since passed into Naval history, Leading Signalman Black had many memories of her and her company, many of whom would by now be dead in the natural course of time even if they hadn't been killed at sea in the subsequent actions of the 1914–18 war, and there was something about that strange signal that made it all seem personal to himself.

Before standing down from action stations, Morgan had asked the Captain if he intended making any report to NOIC Falkland Islands.

'What about?' Cameron asked. 'We saw nothing.' He sounded edgy and realized it himself. He had hazarded his ship for no purpose; the fact that they had come through intact didn't override the thoughts about what might have happened. They could have gone down like a stone, with no possibility of rescue for those not killed in the impact. When the leading telegraphist came up to report Black's information, Cameron found himself infected by the Scot's gloom. Inexplicable things sometimes happened at sea, and he could find no reason why Flag Officer West Africa should make signals to a ship that no longer existed.

Neither could Frazer; but he made a suggestion. 'It's maybe the Japs, sir, trying to create confusion. They're bound to have the recyphering tables at this stage, sir.'

'They wouldn't know *Inflexible*'s call-sign – and wouldn't use it if they did. They'd credit us with the intelligence to know the facts of our own Navy, Frazer.'

'Aye, sir, maybe they would. Maybe.'

Cameron stared at him. 'What's on your mind?'

'It's nothing, sir.'

'You look as though you've seen a ghost, Frazer.'

'I've a feeling maybe we have, sir.'

Cameron gave a short laugh. 'Then don't broadcast your fears,' he said. 'We don't want everyone believing there's something supernatural around.'

'Aye, sir, maybe it's just a wheen o' blethers.'

'You can take it from me it is, Frazer.' When the leading telegraphist had gone below, Cameron remained staring ahead from the bridge, through the murky dark, wondering about that ship that had passed. Most probably it was a merchantman without radar, and *Briar* had never been noticed. On the other hand it could have been a Japanese warship, and her radar could have developed a fault, like *Briar*'s own Asdic. If so, what was she doing? There was only one thing that was clear: in the absence of orders to the contrary, he had to carry on with his mission. And he was left wondering what he might find when he took his ship into the Beagle Channel. Before clearing his mind of the incident, and he forced himself to a realization that it was no more than that really, he was visited by one more thought that was, like Frazer's gloomy prognostications, just a wheen of blethers: the old *Inflexible* wouldn't have had radar either.

5

MORGAN reported, 'Forty miles to go, sir.'

'We should soon be raising the high ground, Pilot.'

Morgan nodded; they should indeed, but the visibility, though improved, was still pretty foul – and, in a way, just as well. There would be less chance of being spotted, if anyone was foolish enough to be around at the bottom of Patagonia – bottom of Tierra del Fuego to be more precise. Morgan shivered and looked sideways at Thompson, who had the morning watch. Thompson was as sleek as ever, though he needed a shave. Not a hair out of place when he pulled back the hood of his duffel-coat to shake off the wetness. How he did it under a duffel-coat hood was a minor miracle; Morgan's sandy thatch was for ever standing on end, like a hedge. Female passengers used to remark on it in his Orient Line days and he used to say it was the way they ruffled it up for him. Currently Morgan was engaged to one of the rufflers and her name was Maria and she happened to come from the Argentine, where her old man was in the inevitable – beef. Plenty of money and he'd spoken of his future son-in-law leaving the sea when the war was over. But not Morgan; he would never leave the sea, especially to go into beef and be under father-in-law's thumb. Nor the Argentine come to that; Morgan was very British, or more specifically very Welsh. There were plenty of Welshmen in the Falkland Islands, sheep men who had gone out generations ago to carve out a better living for themselves when Wales was a

54

depressed land – when hadn't it been ? – and Morgan knew, because Thompson ex-Foreign Office had told him, that the Argentinians had been casting covetous eyes on the Falklands ever since the British flag had been hoisted so long ago.

Well, they would have to go on casting them. But Morgan wouldn't be around to watch. Maria was going to come to England when it was all over, and they would get a house somewhere near Tilbury – Kent or Essex – and she would wait for him to come back every three months from Australia.

Thompson pulled the hood over his head again, smoothing down his hair unnecessarily as he did so. He caught Morgan's sardonic look, and grinned. 'Never know who you're going to meet,' he said. 'Must look smart.'

'That the way to promotion, is it ?'

'It helps.'

'Smarmy bugger.'

Thompson grinned again ; he didn't mind, he was easy, he was a diplomat. He intended to go far in the foreign service and you had to get used to insults, more politely put than Morgan's and on an international scale. Thompson foresaw a lot of tweaking of the lion's tail once this war was over. Assuming Britain won, and that was a reasonably foregone conclusion, the world wouldn't go on wearing the Empire concept, though a lot of people didn't or wouldn't see it. Churchill, for one – it was all very well saying jaw, jaw was better than war, war but good old Winston loved a war nevertheless and was basically incapable of visualizing a day when he couldn't any longer send a gunboat. A whole generation of people was going to have to re-think its attitudes. It was sad but, in Thompson's view, inescapable.

It was more than an hour later when Morgan said, 'I think I've raised land, sir.'

For the hundredth time Cameron lifted his glasses ahead, then nodded. 'I think so too, Pilot. Just a loom through the filth.' He felt a tightening of his guts, a reaction to what might lie close behind the emerging, forbidding landscape, to a time when it would be all up to himself until the sappers were landed to carry out their mission, and then again when they'd done the job. He said, 'Send down to Major Dixon, Thompson. My compliments and I'd like a word with him.'

'Aye, aye, sir.' Thompson gestured at the bridge messenger, Ordinary Seaman Quinn, who had heard what the Captain had said. Quinn slid down the ladder and went aft. The corvette was rolling still, rolling sickeningly to a heavy swell and a confused sea. The wind howled as dismally as ever – more so in fact despite the approaching lee of the land. Not so far off Cape Horn now, the stormy place where the old windjammers had often spent weeks attempting to beat into the westerlies, to find a shift of wind that would carry them on to the calmer waters of the South Pacific. Quinn wouldn't have minded making the east-west passage of the Horn, and wondered how long it had been since one of His Majesty's ships had gone that way. It was real sailoring and it must have been a great sight to see a battleship riding the westerlies in a way that would be impossible for anything under sail.

Cameron's mind was projecting ahead. He had had discussions with Major Dixon and the senior sapper NCO, Staff Sergeant Strong. Dixon and Strong knew their jobs and had laid down what they wanted of the corvette. *Briar* would land the contingent as close as possible to the target area and then lie off for eventual re-embarkation ; and a Naval party under an officer, a petty officer and a leading seaman would land as a protective force with orders to assist the sappers as and when required. Cameron was disinclined to part with his First Lieutenant and equally would have a need of the navigating officer. The choice that was left was between Thompson, Sykes and Midshipman Carruthers ; and it was easy enough. Thompson would go in charge of the Naval party. When this had been announced, the sigh of relief from Sykes had been more than audible. With Thompson would

56

go Petty Officer Gates and Leading Seaman Hoggett plus fifteen mixed able seamen and ordinary seamen and a signal-man with a battery Aldis for communication with the ship.

A clatter of feet on the ladder announced Major Dixon, who saluted formally.

'Morning, Major.' Cameron returned the salute.

'Good morning, Captain. Another filthy day.'

Cameron grinned. 'And likely to remain so.' He waved an arm ahead. 'There you are. Your sphere of operations.'

'Nasty!' Dixon was a tall, gangling man with a mop of black hair and a rather hollow chest that spoke of bronchial trouble. It didn't stop him smoking. He extended a packet of duty-free Players and lit one himself, inhaling deeply. 'What's on your mind?'

Cameron, wedged against the roll in the starboard for'ard corner of the bridge, said, 'That ship that passed us.'

Dixon laughed. 'The ghost ship?'

'No ghost about it,' Cameron said. 'I'm not too happy about it.'

'We've been into that.'

'Yes. But I've done some more thinking ... my W/T people have picked up more signals, all of them originating in Freetown and all addressed to ships that were at the Falklands battle in the last lot – all of them ships that don't appear in the current Navy List, ship names that haven't been repeated. *Inflexible*, *Invincible*, *Canopus*, plus those that were at Coronel under Cradock – *Monmouth* and *Good Hope*.'

'So?'

'There's something odd going on. The only reasonable explanation I can see is that Flag Officer West Africa is trying to make the Japs believe the British are down here in strength – hoping they'll pick up the signals and decypher them.'

Dixon drew on his cigarette. 'D'you know what's in the signals?'

Cameron nodded. 'Yes, I do. I've had them read and broken down. They're a mixture of orders and advice and general guff about stores and returns – you know the sort of thing – '

'Yes indeed. We suffer from bumph too.'

'They're a load of obvious bullshit – obvious to us, that is. Not, presumably, to the Japs.'

'And what's the worry?'

'Just that everything has a reason.'

Dixon laughed again. 'Not as far as the bloody Army's concerned!'

'Well, anyway, I see a possible reason, Major. It's this: either Flag Officer West Africa, or the Admiralty, has got word that the Japs are massing in greater strength than was thought – '

Putting their heart and soul into it?'

'That's right.'

'So Winston's dreamed up one of his wheezes?'

'I don't know about Winston, but someone has.'

Dixon frowned. 'Then why don't they keep us informed? I grant you can't break wireless silence yourself, but you can – and do – receive.'

'It's what I just said – that the Japs can break the cypher. The originator of those signals won't take the risk of addressing us direct with information.'

'H'm . . . ' Dixon pondered, lifting a long chin to scratch reflectively beneath it. 'Those intercepted signals . . . you spoke of orders. Can you tell me what they were, these orders to the ghost ships of 1914?'

'They were orders despatching them to the South Atlantic. To the Falklands.'

'I see. So what you're suggesting is, that ship that whizzed past us could have been a Jap, part of this suspected greater build-up?'

'I think it's possible, in which case – '

'Our job's off?'

'No. We've no orders for that. But we may be heading into a very different situation. You'll have to be prepared for that, Major. Better warn your chaps.' Cameron paused. 'There's another thing: I'll have to play my part by ear. I may not be able to go in as close as we planned – that depends on what we find of a Japanese or neutral presence. We don't want to be seen, you'll appreciate that.'

'Of course. Secrecy's the whole point, obviously. What you mean is, my chaps might be better off sneaking in on their own on the final lap?'

'Yes. With my landing party, of course, but not the ship. I'm sorry, but – '

'That's all right,' Dixon said. 'It's perfectly understood. We're not here for a Christmas party. You take us as far in as appears reasonable and we'll be happy.'

Cameron nodded. 'Thank you, Major.'

'Delighted to oblige. There's just one thing I'd dearly love ... and that is, to lay my charges under the bloody Admiralty and War House and leave a note saying we also serve who only wait for information. Bloody chair-borne warriors!' Dixon turned away and caught Thompson's eye. 'You've been a Whitehall wallah, I'm told. What do you think of them, now you're out here on the other end of the command structure? No, wait – you'd better not say. You'd only fracture something, trying to give a diplomatic answer ....'

In the operations room, the chair-borne warriors were having a difficult time of it. As the Rear-Admiral had remarked earlier, the Prime Minister was taking a personal interest in the safety of the Falkland Islands; the Duty Captain had received some angry telephone calls from Downing Street, such that he had found it necessary to summon the Rear-Admiral from rest. And not solely on account of the Prime Minister.

'Intelligence reports, sir, about the Cape Horn area.'

'Let's have 'em, then.'

The Duty Captain put some typed sheets in front of the Rear-Admiral, who studied them closely then looked up. 'God damn!' he said. 'More bloody yellow perils thought to be converging on that damn southerly maze ... what about the Americans? Have they been informed?'

The Duty Captain indicated the heading on the report sheets. 'The intelligence came from them, sir.'

'Eh? Oh, yes, so it did. What are they doing about it?'

'I don't know yet, sir.'

'Find out, then. The Japanese are said, aren't they, to be still in the Pacific – these reinforcements I mean. The Pacific's a US show. Wait a minute, though.'

'Yes, sir?'

'That frigate, whatsitsname –'

'Corvette. *Briar*.'

'Yes, that's it. I foresee difficulties.'

The Duty Captain considered that to be a monstrous understatement. 'So do I,' he said.

'Their presence, their mission, is more than ever necessary.'

'It's likely to be suicidal in my opinion.'

The Rear-Admiral frowned. 'Don't exaggerate. In any case, war's war. They know the risks.'

'They don't now. The odds may be very greatly increased, sir. I think Cameron should be warned of what to expect –'

'Dammit, *we* don't know what to expect! There's nothing precise in all this, it's largely conjecture.' The Rear-Admiral pushed at the intelligence reports bad-temperedly. 'And Churchill's personal interest ... you know how he tends to want to run the whole blasted Navy – with respect, of course, and that's between you and me. No, I can't risk making signals to *Briar* at this stage, it's all far too delicate. Basically the situation hasn't changed, you know.' He drummed his fingers on his desk. 'I'm really not very worried about –' He broke off as a security telephone gave a gentle burr.

The Duty Captain answered it, then looked across at the Rear-Admiral. 'The Prime Minister,' he said.

'Oh, not *again*!'

Briar was now into the Le Maire Strait and even there the wind blew strong. The cold was bitter; there was no let-up from the spray and the solid water that was flung aboard. She was a little ship and her freeboard was low. As the corvette had entered the twenty-mile-wide strait between Tierra del Fuego and Staten Island Cameron had sent his ship's company to action stations. From now on, anything might happen, and it might happen suddenly. A close lookout was kept on the water ahead and astern and, so far as the binoculars would allow, on the coastlines to port and starboard. The passage through would take a little over three hours; their speed was being cut by the filthy weather and the batter of the westerlies. On emerging she would steam along the rocky coast of Tierra del Fuego, past Aguirre Bay and then north of the island of Nueva to enter the Beagle Channel.

They were a little astern of their projected timing when Morgan said, 'Aguirre Bay, sir, fine on the starboard bow.'

'Thank you, Pilot. From now on we might be spotted. It all depends who by.'

'Shepherd tending sheep, sir?'

'We hope that's all, Pilot! That wouldn't worry me too much.' Cameron glanced aft to where the Naval ensign of the Argentine floated blue-and-white in place of the hauled-down White Ensign. It was some protection, but might not hold for long against any sighting by the neutral armed forces, who might be expected to know the movements of their own warships. Cameron felt in a sadly exposed position as he took the corvette on along the coast; and he was as worried as ever about the purport of the phoney signals that had been made, though the leading telegraphist had reported nothing further since their first sighting of the Patagonian coast.

Even the fact that they had ceased could have its hidden

61

significance. The worries of a Captain were legion : Cameron looked down at the gun's crew on the 4-inch. Their worries were different. They might well be considering life and death, but the odds were heavily that they were not. The British matloe didn't think that way on the whole, and their minds would be mostly occupied with the prospect of mail from home when they got back to Port Stanley, the chances of a run ashore in the Falklands before returning to Freetown, and the doubtful hope of successfully cadging sippers from someone else's daily tot of rum. For them it was a relatively simple life of going on watch and coming off again, of getting their heads down for a spell and then being called by the bosun's mate for another turn on deck. Nose to the grindstone but minds unextended, except for the petty officers who had to chase them and see that the work was done. Three classes aboard a ship : the junior ratings who did the work, the petty officers and leading hands who made sure they did it but didn't work themselves, and the wardroom officers who stood about and watched. And worried. Officers drew their pay to worry, most of all the Captain . . . he was in another class, a class all by himself. Command was a solitary business.

Cameron found himself wondering what his ship's company thought of him. The point was not really an introspective one, it was only sensible to try to get into men's minds and make some assessment of their attitudes. Much could depend on it. A Captain who was trusted implicitly was likely to have not only a better ship's company but also to get a faster reaction to orders, unpopular ones especially, than a Captain who had failed to earn that trust. Cameron, not long in the ship, not much time in which to get to know his sailors fully, could not be sure of how he stood, but had been heartened by the tone and attitude of the senior ratings such as the coxswain, the buffer and the Chief ERA. All men of long experience, each of them more than old enough to be his father, they had seemed to accept him after a natural initial caution. He believed he could see a liking in their faces and hear it in their voices ; but liking was not enough and was not what he sought, although it could be a prerequisite to trust. And to gain trust you had demonstrably to be right whenever you gave an order.

Cameron didn't know whether or not he had passed that acid test. The leaving of the German survivors from that U-boat was weighing on him. He knew Morgan, for one, hadn't liked that. He didn't like it himself, in retrospect. He had allowed anger and hatred to get the better of his mind. That was not what a Captain should do, however natural it might be.

'Beagle Channel ahead, sir.'

Morgan again : Morgan was lynx-eyed, always seemed to spot things before anyone else. Cameron picked up the microphone of the tannoy. 'This is the Captain speaking. We have the Beagle Channel in view now. Full alertness throughout the ship. That is all.' He moved to the engine-room voice-pipe. 'Chief, Captain here. All well below ?'

'All's well, sir ... everything bearing an equal strain as they say, sir.'

'Good. Once we're in the channel, stand by for fast changes of revolutions.'

'Aye, aye, sir.'

Cameron replaced the voice-pipe cover. He wished he didn't have that wretched shake in his fingers. He looked fore and aft, right along his decks, at the men in their stations, watchful, ready. Ready for anything – even Carruthers at the searchlight with Able Seaman Fish, who was scratching beneath his oilskin, face all puckered up as though he was searching for a tiresome flea that kept eluding him. A rumour had gone round the ship earlier, and had not been lost upon the Captain, that Carruthers had gone to sleep during action stations. Well, rumour was a hard thing to work on, but for the sake of his ship's company Cameron had had a discreet word with Carruthers, who had hotly denied any lack of vigilance. Cameron hadn't believed him but had had to take his word. And Carruthers had accused Fish of insolence. This, Cameron had disregarded ; if there had been insolence it would have been to do with the business of sleeping on duty, and some washing was better left in its dirt. But it added to his worries for the future. Perhaps he should have given Carruthers a real bawling out. That might have been good for the ship's company when it reached their ears, as it assuredly would have done, however privately it had been administered ; in any ship, the Captain's steward was a reliable retailer of private information.

The Beagle Channel loomed. *Briar* passed in, to be enclosed by the arms of the land. From now on the wide freedom of the seas was gone. The day seemed to darken even more as the shore at last took the weight out of the wind and a curious half-silence came down.

6

THE sound was distant, its source obscured by the low cloud, but it was coming closer. 'Aircraft,' Cameron said. 'Stand by all guns' crews.'

Morgan passed the order. In a tense silence, they waited. Cameron spoke to the Chief ERA by voice-pipe. 'Aircraft, Chief. I'll keep you informed.'

'Aye, aye, sir.' Parbutt turned away from the voice-pipe and took a long look round his engine-room, which was the smallest he'd ever seen, hardly room to swing a cat and filled with a criss-cross of steam pipes and steel ladders and the vital machinery that drove the shaft, so filled that even a short man had to twist and bend and mind his head to get around. Sometimes you had to move fast and this could be one of those times. Parbutt, ever since joining the corvette, had felt more than a touch of claustrophobia in the engine-room, and never mind his long experience of more-or-less confined spaces. But he acknowledged that down in this cluttered and clattering part of the world at least he was better off than the poor sods up there on deck. It was warm, the only warm part of the ship for many days past and, always in a heavy sea, the only place where the lads could hope to dry out their watch-wet clothing, always provided he was willing to give permission to turn his small kingdom into a Chinese laundry. Being a considerate man, he usually was ; and right now the large waistband of Stripey Fish's blue serge bell-bottoms was wrapped around a steam pipe and gently

cooking. Parbutt wrinkled his nose : wet serge had a nasty
smell.

A few minutes after the first report from the bridge, the
Captain called down again. 'Passed over, Chief.'

Parbutt said, 'Thanks for letting us know, sir. Did we get
spotted ?'

'I don't know for sure. But I'll have to assume we were.'

'Right, sir. Any special orders ?'

'Not for now, Chief. I'll maintain the speed for the time
being.' Cameron stood back from the voice-pipe, his face
anxious. The aircraft had looked like a reconnaissance job
and it had come low, emerging from the cloud base only very
briefly before passing on to become enveloped again. Even
its markings remained unidentified but Cameron felt
justified in deciding it wasn't likely to be Japanese ; if it was,
they would have needed to get a carrier right down south and
Cameron believed the United States would have known
about the movement of Jap aircraft-carriers and would have
informed the Admiralty. So the thing had to be either
Chilean or Argentinian, neither of which neutral countries
would welcome a belligerent entering their waters. But that
had been a risk all along.

Morgan said, 'If they did spot us, sir, they'll have seen the
Argentine ensign.'

'Perhaps. But when they check the ship movements they'll
smell a rat.' Cameron rubbed hard at his eyes ; he was dead
tired and his eyes were smarting from lack of sleep and con-
stant vigilance. 'How much further in the Beagle Channel,
Pilot ?'

Morgan's response was immediate. 'Off the island in just
under an hour, sir. We could do the job and be bound east
again inside about what, four hours.'

'If there's no interference.'

'It's a chance either way,' Morgan said.

'I know. I've half a mind to get lost somewhere among the
inlets . . . just till the scare dies down.'

'We don't know there *is* a scare, sir. Not for sure.'

'No, you're right, Pilot. Very well, we'll press on till something shows more positively. But in the meantime, we'll have a look at the chart.'

'Right, sir. Find a funk-hole?'

Cameron gave a tight grin. 'Call it that if you like, Pilot. But I don't want the mission to abort just because of interference from bloody neutrals.'

'There's a question of time involved, remember.'

'I'm aware of that.' Cameron kept his voice cool, but irritation was beginning to mount. Morgan was a first-class navigator and a good all-round officer as well, but there was an abrasiveness about him and a touch of the cocksure as well. He had a master mariner's certificate and Cameron had not. Cameron, whose father had been a master mariner, knew all about that. There lay the difference between the two Naval reserves, the qualified and the unqualified. Cameron knew that it rankled with Morgan. That was all very well and he was prepared to concede the point; but a master's certificate was a guarantee of professional seamanship competence and not of any inbuilt ability to make tactical decisions in war. That was the Captain's job and he was the Captain. Seamanship qualifications didn't enter into it.

Morgan seemed to sense a stiffness in the air. He said, 'I spoke out of turn, sir. I apologize.'

Cameron waved a hand. 'That's all right, Pilot, we won't fall out over it. I've got time well in mind, believe me. But it's better to accept some delay rather than have to call it all off – right?'

Morgan nodded. 'We'll just have to hope the Japs don't move through first, that's all.' He wasn't convinced; with Cameron he moved to the chart table. There were any number of inlets, some navigable, some not. It would be easy enough for a small warship to lie hidden, at any rate until someone ordered a full-scale search and even then the maze element would work in their favour. A search would take a long time and they might even be able to keep one jump ahead. Morgan said, putting the tip of a pair of dividers on the chart, 'There, sir. That's where I'd go.'

Cameron looked. 'Doesn't seem to have a name.'

'They'd run out of ideas if they tried to name everything round here. All right, sir? It's pretty well enclosed by the mountains.'

The inlet led off a side channel running south from the Beagle Channel into Nassau Bay. That, Cameron said, would do well enough if they had to use it. 'Sufficient water for us,' Morgan said, 'but not for anything much bigger. I just hope we don't need to use it, sir.'

'Anxious to get out to sea?' Cameron asked. 'If so, you're not the only one.'

Morgan nodded but said nothing further. He didn't like these waters; they were a navigator's nightmare at the best of times and not, in fact, much used on that account. Besides which – perhaps it was his Welsh blood – he was still thinking about that unknown ship. Superstition was bunk, of course, but . . . well, it was a weird set of circumstances and Morgan didn't like it. Superstition was deep in a good many seamen. Once, in an Orient liner, a fool of a passenger, mucking about with a shotgun in the Great Australian Bight, had shot and killed an albatross and the Captain had almost gone berserk, though he was normally a hard-headed man. He'd put the passenger in arrest for a while and the company had backed him afterwards when a complaint went in. Albatrosses, after all, were the repositories of the souls of seafarers dead and gone. . . .

'There it is again,' Morgan said, breaking away from his dafter thoughts. 'Hear it, sir?'

'Yes,' Cameron answered. 'Warn the guns' crews again.' He leaned over the fore rail and himself called down to Thompson, officer of the quarters on the 4-inch. 'Coming back in,' he said.

'Do we open, sir?'

'Not if we can help it – same as last time. Just stand by for orders.' Cameron sweated beneath his thick clothing. It wouldn't do to fire on a neutral and create diplomatic panic back in nice, safe Whitehall. Everything would have to depend on the aircraft's own actions. Cameron didn't expect actual attack, just a buzzing. On the other hand, it just could turn out to be a Jap after all; they *could* have brought a carrier down to cover their assault force. Cameron found himself cursing through set teeth: what he needed was information, something to go on. He was working in the dark, having to make guesses that might be all too wildly off the mark.

The engine sounds grew louder and, as last time, the aircraft appeared very suddenly from the murk, once again flying low – lower this time. Lower and, since it was below the cloud base for longer, more visibly.

A shout came from the leading signalman. *'Jap, sir! Bloody Jap!'*

'Open fire,' Cameron said. He gripped the rail tight, staring up as the aircraft made a run across his bows from north to south. There was a sharp crack from the 4-inch, a stutter of fire from the pom-pom and the 20-mm close-range weapons. No hits: the plane, a fighter-reconnaissance aircraft as was now seen, vanished into the cloud. Then it came back and once again an umbrella of fire was put up. This time the Jap came in with its machine-guns firing. Dots of flame were seen as the aircraft, still keeping low, came slap across the corvette. Bullets sputtered into the upperworks, swept the bridge. By some miracle all the bridge personnel escaped injury; the only damage was to the azimuth circle on the compass. Amidships at the pom-pom the gunlayer hung limply dead over the guardrail, another man lay on the deck, dying, gasping for air with a bullet through his throat, blood pouring. At the unrequired searchlight Stripey Fish put a hand on Carruthers' arm and shouted in his ear.

'Come on, sir. You know the orders, don't you?' The searchlight's crew, when not otherwise needed, were available to shift to the pom-pom and replace casualties; but the midshipman was staring at the bodies and looking sick. Stripey gave him a shove towards the pom-pom and, himself stepping over the dying man, began heaving the other body clear. Carruthers retched and stood there like a dummy. Pinner was a very long way off but it stood clear in his mind, representing sanity. Tennis clubs, boating, sherry parties and bowler-hatted city gents going off on the eight-fifteen while he lay in bed, dreaming of when he would find a woman to share it. No war, no guns, no gruesome dead. Carruthers began to shake uncontrollably, his face as white as a shroud. He was scarcely aware of the buffer coming up behind him.

Lamprey said in a quiet hiss into his ear, 'For Christ's sake. Pull yourself together, Mr Carruthers, before you bloody falls apart. Give Fish a 'and – come on!'

Once again Carruthers was shoved forward. Stripey Fish, doing his best with a heavy deadweight, was swearing like a sergeant of dragoons. Lamprey assisted him; Carruthers was only in the way and had to be disregarded as a useful hand. Fish heaved his gut into the gunlayer's position and lined himself up for a bash as soon as the Jap came in again. Lamprey took the place of the other casualty. As he did so, the aircraft came in for another run and soon after that the First Lieutenant came aft along the deck below the pom-pom mounting.

'You there,' he called up. 'Mid!'

Carruthers turned. 'Yes, sir?'

'Get for'ard, take over OOQ on the 4-inch. Thompson's bought it.' Frome went on aft. Carruthers, shaking like a jelly, started to clamber down from the pom-pom platform, his legs like putty. Damn the war ... if he didn't obey Number One's order he'd be for it in a big way and he didn't know which was worse. Fate, however, intervened, kindly for once. Carruthers lost his footing and crash-landed on the deck with his right leg curling beneath him. He believed the leg was broken; the result was agony and he gave a high scream, but at least it was an honourable way out of a dilemma. Carruthers dragged himself along the deck until he was under the lee of the seaboat at the davits.

A little later, he didn't know how long, he heard cheering; this was followed by a sight of thick, trailing smoke just below the cloud and then, after a short interval, an explosion somewhere on the starboard side

Stock was taken. No one doubted Stripey Fish's claim that it had been him who had got the Jap. A stream of pom-pom shells had gone into the aircraft and that had been that. Fish was a hero; Cameron sent for him and congratulated him and Fish glowed though he tried to act the simple, modest seaman.

'I dunno, sir. Any one o' the lads, they'd have done the same, sir.'

'I realize that. But it was you who pressed the tit, Fish. So well done.'

'Thank you, sir, I does me best, sir.' So mortified had Stripey been that any officer could behave as the midshipman had behaved that he almost added, 'Not like some,' but bit the words back with an effort. Poor little bugger, not long out of school, didn't know what had hit him when he went to war. Maybe he'd learned a lesson; maybe not. Stripey Fish knew that it wasn't always the first time in action that was the worst – you didn't always get used to it, not by a long chalk. Memories of the first time could make each succeeding time worse. Anyway, the middy was out of it now by all accounts. You couldn't fight with a broken leg and he could stay tucked up all nice and comfy in clean sheets next time. Fish left the bridge, smirking a little as he met Petty Officer Gates on the upper deck, expecting a touch of hero worship – it wasn't every bleeding day an AB got brought before the skipper to be told what a good hand he was, that he'd saved the ship and all.

Gates gave him a sardonic look. 'Don't let it go to your 'ead, Stripey.'

'Well, I like that, I must say!' Fish was indignant; trust a PO to rob a man of his glory. 'I'm not boasting, mind, but – '

'Can't reckon out 'ow you 'ad room to get between the gun and the guardrail with that enormous gut,' Gates said, prodding at Fish's stomach.

Fish gave a snort and lumbered aft.

From the bridge Cameron watched the body of Sub-Lieutenant Thompson being carried below. There would now be the question of the disposal of the dead, three of them. Another decision ... Cameron detested the thought of leaving them in these waters, but when you came to think about it, did it really matter? To the ship's company it probably would; seamen always liked decency in committal and were certainly not to be blamed for that. But bodies kept aboard were not popular either; superstition again. In the meantime the weather was icy cold and it might not be necessary to put them in the meat store if he decided to hang on to them until they were out at sea again.

Frome came up to put the very question. Cameron temporized. He said, 'They stay aboard till I've decided, Number One. There's something more urgent for now: with Thompson gone, we have to detail someone else for the landing-party. I reckon it's Hobson's Choice. I can't spare anyone but Sykes.'

Frome pulled a long face. He offered to go himself, but Cameron vetoed that. When it came down to hard fact, Frome had no more experience of landing-parties than had Sykes, and he was better employed aboard.

Sykes hadn't gone much on Thompson and his first thought when he learned that the sub was dead was that the Foreign Office had lost a shining light, ha-ha, I don't think ... but

72

then the fact came home to him that he, Sykes, would now be in line for the landing-party. The midshipman was *hors de combat*, lucky little swine, and he knew Morgan couldn't be spared, or wouldn't be spared, by the Captain. Likewise Frome ; the RN never did get the dirty jobs. So Sykes busied himself in trying to dream up some convincing reason why he shouldn't be landed with the sappers – if in the end it did come to that ; he hoped fervently that it wouldn't, that the advent of the Japanese aircraft had pulled the plug out of a suicide mission and Cameron would lie low, bugger off as soon as possible or, if it went that way, surrender to *force majeure*. Sykes had no wish to end up as a Jap POW but there might be some way in which Cameron could surrender to the Chileans or the Argentinians and then they would all be interned in comparative comfort and for them, as the Jerries said, the war would be over.

It was a nice thought and it could come off. But in the meantime Sykes couldn't think of a reason to offer why he would be useless in charge of the landing-party. He had more than a suspicion that the Captain already knew he would be a dead loss, but had no alternative. If that was indeed the case, then it was pointless even to go on thinking.

Armageddon came : Sykes was summoned to the bridge. He went up with a sinking heart.

'Ah, Sykes. You know the casualties. That leaves you to go with the landing-party, all right ?'

'If you say so, sir – '

'I do, Sykes.'

'Yes, sir,' Sykes coughed. 'I've never been away in charge before – '

'I know that. There's always a first time, isn't there ?' Cameron spoke pleasantly, though he knew what was going on in Sykes' mind. In Cameron's there was contempt. 'You've had basic experience of responsibility in general – '

'Not very much, sir. I – '

'Don't interrupt me,' Cameron said crisply. 'I was

referring to Woolworth's as a matter of fact. Not an easy job to take charge of all those women, I imagine – yet you did it, and I presume you did it satisfactorily. Just don't worry about a thing.'

Sykes looked momentarily flattered, though reflection was to tell him that the Captain was being sardonic; even Sykes could scarcely compare the peacetime Woolworth's routine with the exigencies of war, nor counter girls with horny-handed seamen. But he was unable to think of anything to say in response other than, 'Yes, sir.'

'Good,' Cameron said. He passed the detailed orders and added, 'Have a word with Petty Officer Gates and the rest of the landing-party as soon as you leave the bridge, all right?'

'Yes, sir,' Sykes paused, feeling fear mount already. 'What about, in particular?'

Cameron stared.

'I mean, I – I understood they already knew the orders.'

'Yes, they do. But Thompson was to go. Now it's up to you to establish yourself as their leader. I hope you understand the importance of that, Sykes.'

'Oh – yes, sir.'

'Get on with it, then.' Cameron turned away, hoping against hope that Sykes would put up a reasonable show. Lives would be in his hands – but Gates would be there as ramrod. Gates was thoroughly dependable, according to the First Lieutenant, and Cameron had already formed his own good opinion of the Quarterdeck Division PO. He was one of the very few active service ratings aboard – active service in the Naval phrase as opposed to having been recalled from reserve, though God knew they were all on active service in wartime – and he was comparatively young and dead keen. He would sum up a situation fast, faster in fact than Thompson would have done. Cameron, searching the skies for more aircraft, reflected that it was a sad state of affairs that allowed so many officers to be carried along by the senior ratings of the lower deck, men who would take years to gain commissions if ever they did at all, which was unlikely. If those senior ratings hadn't been loyal, it could have given rise to some very bolshie thoughts. As it was they just sucked their teeth a bit now and again and got on with the job . . . .

The sky, so far as could be seen and heard, remained clear, but Cameron believed it was unlikely to remain so for long. He had still to decide his future movements : did he or did he not head for the target area direct and take a chance in the interest of speed of execution ?

The answer had to be no.

He spoke over his shoulder. 'Pilot.'

'Sir ?'

'We head for that inlet of yours.'

'Aye, aye, sir.' Morgan sounded expectant of the order in the circumstances. 'Shall I take her, sir ?'

'Yes, please, Pilot.' Cameron moved to the tannoy and flicked the switch. 'This is the Captain . . . the ship is proceeding into cover for the time being and although I may land the sapper party I shall not move *Briar* into the target area yet. Further information will be passed to you as soon as possible.' He paused. 'From now on we're in continuing danger, if I need to tell you that. The ship will remain at action stations and there is to be full vigilance on the part of all hands. That is all.'

He switched off. In the comparative silence of the enclosed waters, where the wind was a distant buffet over the mountainous terrain, he heard a buzz of conversation from the 4-inch crew just for'ard of his position. Where Carruthers should have been in charge . . . Carruthers lacked self-confidence, as though too well aware that he had nothing to buttress himself *vis-à-vis* older men other than the maroon midshipman's patches on his lapels. Midshipmen, always the lowest form of animal life in the Royal Navy . . . yet the RN midshipmen, the wearers of white patches, were in most cases older than their years and well able to take charge ; it was the training that counted. You couldn't blame Carruth-

75

ers, his life had been too soft, and very likely his parents too indulgent. Cameron, who came from the granite city of Aberdeen, had known little indulgence either at home or at school. His father had been, still was, a hard man, though just. That had helped, as the old man had known it would. The transition from peace to war had not been unduly hard in Cameron's case. No, you couldn't blame Carruthers. But woe betide him all the same if when his leg was mended, which was way ahead yet, his faint heart ever became the cause of unnecessary casualties.

The W/T signal was received aboard *Briar* just as Morgan was taking her into the narrow tongue of water north of Nassau Bay. The Rear-Admiral in the Admiralty's operations room had had his hand forced when fresh word had come and he had been obliged to pass additional orders by Naval cypher to the corvette and take a chance that the Japanese would not as yet have broken the new recyphering tables just a day or two in force throughout the British Fleet. Cyphers had to be broken down into plain language by officers, not ratings; and when the message was reported to the bridge, Cameron sent it down to Carruthers with orders to get busy on decyphering. An injured leg didn't preclude paperwork. Carruthers had assisted Thompson in this task and had made a fair fist at it. He sent the result of his labours back to the bridge.

Cameron read: *Briar from Admiralty. US Pacific Fleet withdrawn northwards leaving Japanese line of retreat open westwards. On completion of original mission you are to carry out similar orders in rear of enemy squadron. For information Japanese believed repeat believed reinforced with more cruisers.*

7

MORGAN said, 'They're off their collective rocker. The Admiralty, sir. The Japs could go out astern via half a bloody hundred channels!'

Cameron nodded. 'True enough. But those are the orders, Pilot. We'll have a look at the chart.'

'Waste of time, sir. Which do we choose? We can't lay charges all over the whole area between Cape Horn and Punta Arenas –'

'I don't suggest we can. But the field's narrowed quite considerably – once the Japs are nicely in the narrows where the first charges go up. Don't you see? We lay charges right behind them and pen them in.'

'How? D'you mean both sets of charges will be laid at the same time?'

'Yes. With a long land gap between, of course. The Japs steam into a prepared trap – anyway, that's how I reckon Dixon will see it. Now – that chart, Pilot.'

He went with Morgan to the chart table; by the time the midshipman had broken down the cypher, *Briar* had made her entry and was lying off in deep water under the lee of towering peaks, snow-covered and remote, broodingly silent and savage. Morgan said, 'It's going to be like trying to catch a bird with a piece of string and a sieve.'

'I've done that before too,' Cameron said. He studied the chart. It would be the devil's own job and they would need a lot of luck to get two sets of charges laid in time but orders

77

were not to be argued with, the more so as he couldn't break wireless silence to start the argument. And there was another point: here in this enclosed inlet he would be unlikely to receive any further signals. The last one had come just in time as it happened, just before the corvette had gone into the lee of the mountains. As it was, Carruthers had reported difficulty; there had been a large number of corrupt groups, inevitable when there were hills around to distort reception.

It was not long before the buzz had gone round the ship; Cameron had intended to broadcast the information as promised but the galley wireless beat him to it.

The Americans were pulling out.

Why?

'I reckon,' Leading Seaman Hoggett said, 'there's a threat up north. Maybe the bloody Japs castin' eyes at Hawaii or some such, eh?'

'Leaves *us* up the creek whatever it is, killick. P'raps they've gorn back for their perishin' medals.' Stripey Fish scratched reflectively. Yanks ... well, they were unlikely to be bothering his old woman back in Blighty, she wasn't much to look at wasn't Em, but what the boys back home said was true enough: the Yanks, they were overpaid, oversexed and over here. There were some who didn't like the Americans, not appreciating the magnificent help willingly given by President Roosevelt, not appreciating the blood they had shed. Stripey Fish was one of these.

He reckoned they'd had it easy. In the meantime the British Fleet had kept the seas, day in, day out ... *that line of storm-tossed, distant British ships* ... old Napoleon had known what he'd been up against and what had finally beaten him. Stripey Fish quite fancied himself as one of Nelson's tars, coming back to Pompey all war- and weather-battered, back from glory to the fleshpots and the women, down by Point with open arms, and buckshee brandy nicked from the Frogs. He said as much to Ordinary Seaman Beaner, who

78

remarked that at least he'd have been useful ballast aboard the old wooden walls. Leading Seaman Hoggett stepped in to prevent Beaner's sudden death and soon after this the skipper came on the tannoy, but he didn't quell the mutters on the lower deck. Or the wardroom either, come to that. And he left an uneasy feeling behind him when he switched off the tannoy. Plugging one hole against the enemy was fair enough, if highly dangerous, but then to go round his arse and plug the other, that was asking something.

'Can it be done?' Cameron asked the sapper major. 'What I mean is, have you the explosive to do it?'

Dixon shrugged. 'That all depends. Till I set the charges, I can't be sure how much I'm going to need.'

'Why's that?'

'The kind of land – the terrain, the configuration. Your Admiralty Sailing Directions plus some bumph from the War Office are all I've got to go on. I have to see it for myself.'

'But you'll have brought enough to cope with the unexpected, surely?'

'Yes, of course.'

'Double the quantity?'

Dixon grinned. 'Yes. Plus a bit.'

'Well, then – '

'We'll have to wait and see. I'll keep it in mind, no promises.'

'The orders – '

Dixon lifted two fingers in a not quite Churchillian gesture. '*That* to the orders. They weren't given by sappers – I'm not being disrespectful to Their Lordships, or mutinous either, but they don't know any more about explosives than my grandmother knew about contraception. If both had known a little more, then in neither case would I be here now. I've already told you, I think the whole thing's crazy right from the start.'

Cameron grinned. 'Yes, you did mention it, Major.' He

79

had, very vociferously. His sappers had the skill, all right, but to bring down enough rock to hem ships in was a pretty doubtful proposition and couldn't be done quickly.

Dixon asked, 'When do we go in? Sooner the better if you ask me.'

'I agree. And the answer's right now, Major. But you're going to have a long walk. I'll have you put ashore as soon as you're ready. You'd better have a look at the chart.' With Cameron, Dixon went across to the chart table and traced a route from the corvette's current position, over land and water to the island where the first group of charges would be laid. The Army equipment included some collapsible rubber dinghies; and a shuttle service, aided by *Briar*'s whaler for the first water crossing, would be run to the shore. That should prove simple enough; one of the problems of the overland part of the route was going to be the transportation of the explosive material, no light weight, a problem that had not been anticipated since the corvette was to have taken the sappers close up to the target area. There was no way round this other than to let Dixon use the Naval ratings to help hump all the gear by hand; and already Sykes had been told of this.

Dixon stood back from the chart. 'All ready.' He leaned over the bridge rail and called down. 'Staff, get the chaps mustered right away. We're landing now.'

'Very good, sir.' Staff Sergeant Strong saluted and moved off.

Cameron said, 'Swing out the seaboat, Number One, and send down to Sykes.' Frome left the bridge, sliding on his palms down the ladder's handrail. Sykes, who was on deck and muffled to the eyebrows, was told to get his party fallen in pronto. Sykes passed the word to Petty Officer Gates and did something cack-handed with his issued revolver, managing to point it at Gates as he was speaking to him.

Gates executed a smart nip aside and asked politely, 'Is that ruddy thing loaded by any chance, sir?'

80

'Er – yes, it is.'

'I see, sir. I take it, of course, you've used one before, sir?'

'Oh, yes,' Sykes lied.

Gates didn't believe him for a moment; no one but a bloody lunatic, if he knew what he was about, would wave a loaded revolver in the air like a kid with a rattle. Gates said, 'Well, sir, if you don't want to have to report to the skipper that you've gone and shot the landing-party before the Japs have had a go . . . well, if I was you, sir, I'd unload till you see a need, all right?'

Sykes flushed. Damn the blasted war. His fingers were shaking as he took the offered advice and started to slip the cartridges out of the chambers. 'Here, let me,' Gates said, risking his life. He took the revolver and unloaded with speed and efficiency. 'Got a holster, sir?' he asked.

'Yes. Somewhere . . .' Sykes fuffled about inside his warm clothing and finally got there. Gates clicked his tongue but said nothing further. It wouldn't be his fault if the daft ha'porth had to undress before he could fire. Sykes needed a nursemaid, not a seaman PO. Chances were, he'd made a right cock of Woolworth's store and they couldn't wait to see the back of him when he was called up and God help King George thereafter. But he looked like being easy meat, kind of malleable, and wouldn't argue the toss if he, Gates, had to take charge in the event of his seeing an almighty balls-up approaching. Gates doubted if Mr Sykes would know a balls-up from a fried egg. It was useless articles like Sykes who shook confidence in the RNVR. The vast majority of them did at least try and in the end grew efficient, like the skipper. . . .

When Sykes had sorted himself out the landing of the naval party and the sappers with all their equipment proceeded, watched from the bridge by Cameron. It took three trips of the seaboat to get them all ashore; the leaden skies remained clear of aircraft throughout. As the seaboat came back to be hoisted and secured after its final run the sound of engines was heard but nothing showed; it was a time for breath-holding and crossed fingers. The sounds grew fainter; the ship's cover was good. Frome came to the bridge to report formally that the landing-parties had been put ashore.

'Right, Number One. Now we just wait.'

'Not easy, sir.'

'You're telling me! It's the worst time of all – it always is.' War, Cameron knew by this time, was largely a waiting game. Waiting for information, waiting for the enemy to show himself, waiting for him to establish his intentions. It was all right when you were under way, for instance with a convoy; you still waited for the U-boat attacks and the dive-bombers but at least you had a distance to chalk up each day, more miles put behind to your destination. Waiting with engines stopped, waiting for someone else to do the dirty work and then come back, that was a kind of hell. It meant that time seemed to stand still; you watched the clock and the fact of watching it made the hands crawl like slugs. And all the time you thought about the many things that could go wrong and the sad fact, so often, was that the thing that did go wrong was the one thing you hadn't taken into account so you were caught on the hop. *For want of a nail a shoe was lost, for want of a shoe a horse was lost, for want of a horse a battle was lost.* That was the way things went. The mind of a CO boggled at the immensity of the computations. . . .

Frome went down to the upper deck. He at least had something positive to do; First Lieutenants, nannies of the entire ship, always had. All the departments brought their troubles and their requests to the First Lieutenant, none more frequently than the chief bosun's mate, PO Lamprey.

'First Lootenant, sir – '

'Yes, Buff?'

''Ammicks and bedding, sir. Time they was aired on deck. Grab a moment when it's not raining or snowing, sir.'

'I'm afraid they'll have to wait.'

'Gettin' a bit thick below, sir.' Lamprey wrinkled his

nose ; Frome sympathized. Nightly rounds of the ship had become a time of pong, even though one passed quickly enough through the messdecks. What it must be like for those who had to sleep in it . . . Frome said, 'Can't be done. Blankets and mattresses flapping about on deck might attract attention if anything flies over the inlet.'

Lamprey nodded. It had been worth a try but he knew Jimmy was right. He coughed ; he had something else on his mind. 'How long do we have to wait, sir ?'

Frome said, 'The Captain's given them twelve hours, which is on the generous side. If they're not back by then, we move round to the island.'

'Pick 'em up, sir ?'

Frome nodded. 'We hope so, Buff, we hope so.' In point of fact, if the landing-parties failed to return on time, anything could have happened. The sounds of any fighting in the meantime might not be heard ; the land configuration in parts of the world such as this could play funny buggers with the acoustics. But Frome had already raised the point with the Captain. If hostile noises should be heard from the vicinity of the landing area, *Briar* would at once get under way and move, like Kipling's wild geese, to the sound of the guns.

Frome moved on along the deck accompanied by the buffer. If he was a nanny, he was the ship's housemaid as well. Routinely, his eye noted part-of-ship details – paintwork, a bent stanchion, rust on the gun-shields. Back at base, the chipping hammers would have to be set to work. Even in wartime a ship had to be kept as tiddley as possible.

Ordinary Seaman Beaner, struggling along with a ruddy great mass of explosive material dangling around his skinny body, was taking it all in his stride and keeping happy by not paying any particular attention to the war and his current situation. He was thinking of home and the girl his mum didn't like, Alice. That was the way to get through the hard times – by disregarding them and filling the mind with something nice. Beaner wasn't in the waters behind Cape Horn, he was mooching along Lovers' Lane and wondering what the chances would be if he took a risk, found a quiet spot and made a real dive for it. His mum's assessment of Alice had been dead wrong; Beaner, who had made some tentative moves on occasion, had reason to know that what his mum called the tarty appearance didn't go even skin deep. Alice was extraordinarily prudish and guarded everything like the crown jewels, always anticipating his moves and being ready to parry his hands with one of hers.

Talk about frustration. There was a name for girls like Alice, the ones who made themselves up to look as though they couldn't wait for it and then when the moment came put their guard up. Perhaps, next leave, he'd find someone more co-operative. If he did, the chances were that she'd look mousy and sexless, which would please his mum and make life that much easier. It was a funny thing about women: they never looked the part they meant to play, not unless they were actually on the game anyway, and Beaner wouldn't touch prozzies, not at any price. Much too risky. He'd heard some hair-raising stories. If you got a dose, and you were bound to, and left it too long, all your hair fell out and your flesh got gradually eaten away like by rats. You became a sort of leper, shunned by all. It was only a question of time before all the prozzies got eaten away but there were always plenty more to take their places and set their snares for the unwary.

'You there – Beaner!'

Beaner came back to his surroundings as Gates' voice smote through the daydream. 'Yes, PO?'

'Bloody keep up! Arse-end Charlie, that's you, Beaner.'

'Sorry, PO.' Beaner put on a bit of speed; he was carrying a lot of weight and it had bent his tall body almost in two. He came abreast of Quinn, who somehow managed to keep fit at sea and wasn't bothered by his load. Quinn was one of the dead keen ones, the sort who volunteered, daft prat. Home had now been broken into and for some reason or other

84

Beaner couldn't get back to it and he began to suffer and moan.

'Bloody carry-on this is, eh.'

'At least we're doing something.'

'Who wants to do anything?'

Quinn grinned. 'What you joined for, isn't it?'

'No. I joined because I bloody had to. They can stuff this lark, mate.' Beaner blew out his breath. 'Who's in charge? That Army bloke, or Sykes?'

'Army, overall.'

'Thank Christ for that.'

Gates was right behind them in more ways than one, but automatically kept the discipline going when he overheard remarks like that. 'Shut your trap, Beaner. Any more o' that and I'll have you in the rattle.'

He moved on, marching briskly up the laden line, left-right-left so far as the terrain would allow. It was quite a sight. Beaner gave a sardonic laugh and said, 'Stupid git should have been a gunner's mate, all bull and bang me arse.'

Way ahead, Gates drew level with Sub-Lieutenant Sykes and gave him a sideways look.

'All right, sir, are we?'

Sykes looked half dead. Breathlessly he said, 'It's a bit of a strain I must admit.'

'*You*'re not carrying anything, sir. It's the lads that have the load. They need encouragement, sir.'

Sykes' face went red. The remark had been pointed. He said, 'Are you suggesting something, Petty Officer Gates?'

'Me, sir? Oh, no, sir! Not my place, is it, to do that? Wouldn't dream of it, sir.' Gates sounded too damn cheerful, Sykes thought savagely. Gates remained at the officer's side for a while, still marching briskly and forcing Sykes to do the same. Gates felt some satisfaction; his words had made a small penetration of a thick hide – Sykes had to have a thick hide or he'd never have had the bleeding cheek to offer himself for a commission in the first place – and the result lay

85

in a small smartening-up of his bearing. Shoulders back, stomach in and he began to look more like a man than a muffled-up grandma with her revolver still buried under the layers of wool.

Cameron took the opportunity of the current inaction to leave the bridge in Morgan's hands and go below for a word of cheer to Midshipman Carruthers. Carruthers was lying on his bunk, restored to him after he'd been injured, with his leg swathed in bandages applied with the splints by the sick-berth attendant who was the corvette's sole medical authority.

'How's it going, Mid?' Cameron grinned from the cabin doorway.

'Painful, sir.'

'Stupid thing to have done.'

'Yes, sir. I'm awfully sorry, sir.'

'I wasn't criticizing unduly, Mid,' Cameron said. 'But you should have remembered the old sailing-ship dictum: one hand for the ship and one for yourself.'

'Yes, sir. I'm sorry to be a nuisance, sir. Sorry to miss what's going on,' he added unconvincingly. 'I don't like being a deadweight, sir.'

'We'll survive,' Cameron said. Carruthers, he thought, looked anguished more by the bare discomfort of his surroundings than by what he was depriving the ship of. Had his leg been broken in Pinner, or was it Northwood, he would have been pampered in the lap of luxury, with the services of a private nurse and daily visits by a doctor. Mummy and Daddy would have spared no effort to keep him amused. He had a petulant, childish look, baby-face lying sick in bed. Outside, men were enduring real hardship and probably marching into danger. Cameron stifled a sigh of exasperation and was about to offer a final word of consolation when the sharp crack of the 4-inch echoed throughout the ship.

8

CAMERON was on the bridge within thirty seconds. Morgan said, 'No time to send down for you, sir –'

'That's all right.' Cameron had seen the situation for himself : a small warship had appeared in the entrance to the inlet, a ship of about their own size wearing the Japanese Naval ensign. As Cameron trained his binoculars on her, there was a flash and a shell took the water a little way off the corvette's starboard side. A small waterspout went up, sent spray flying over the bridge. The 4-inch was pumping away to good effect : a hit was observed on the Japanese ship's port bow and when the smoke and flame burst out Cameron saw a gaping hole in her side above the waterline. Not mortal damage, but it showed that *Briar*'s gunners had the range right. After that more shells found their mark ; within a matter of a minute and a half the Japanese bridge was seen to be burning and hanging off to port. Something had landed in the superstructure beneath.

'We've got smack inside her wheelhouse,' Cameron said. The Japanese gun was still in action but the shambles behind them seemed to have affected the gunners and the aim was poor. *Briar* took no hits at all. Then a shell took the Japanese on her fo'c'sle, there was a blinding flash and a roar and the gun blew into fragments, fragments that must have knifed through what was left of the gun's crew.

Cameron said, 'Cease firing.' He bent to the voice-pipe. 'Full ahead main engine, wheel amidships.' He straightened.

'She's staying afloat by the look of it, Pilot. She mustn't get away.'

'Cut her off, sir?'

'Yes. And I want some men left alive for questioning.'

Morgan said, 'Let's hope some of the sods speak English, then. I doubt if we have any Japanese speakers, somehow.'

Cameron, staring ahead as the corvette moved towards the entrance, made no response. He was assessing the chances; he might have to open fire again or he might not. Maybe there was a better way than point-blank firing at close range. He took up the tannoy, then put it down again. Speech could carry. He spoke down the voice-pipe.

'Cox'n ... pass to the buffer, all seamen to muster, port side fore and aft, with rifles and bayonets. Fast as you can. I'm going to lay alongside and board.'

'Aye, aye, sir!' Chief Petty Officer Rodman was grinning to himself as he sent a bosun's mate post-haste to find the buffer. Boarding ... that was real Nelson stuff and didn't often happen, not in this war, not since Captain Vian had taken the *Cossack* alongside the POW ship *Altmark* in Jossing Fjord. Rodman's grin was one of anticipation; in his early days in the Andrew, back before the last war, he'd been trained as a Seaman Boy First class in cutlass drill and now he would have liked nothing better than to leap aboard the Jap and swing cold steel to slice through necks and see the heads roll in the scuppers, not that it would be quite like that today – just bullets topped up with a few bayonet thrusts. A lot of the old-time colour had gone out of the Navy, but never mind. Rodman gripped the wheel tight as the little *Briar* went on at her best speed, closing the gap.

On the bridge Cameron saw that the Jap was moving astern; a swirl of churned-up water moved for'ard past her bows, then she began to swing a little. She would be using emergency steering. But *Briar* was closing the gap nicely, and within the next five minutes was coming round the enemy's stern and lying across the inlet's entry channel.

Cameron said, 'Port ten.'

'Port ten, sir. Ten of port wheel on, sir.'

'Engine to half ahead.'

'Engine to half ahead, sir.' Bells rang below. 'Engine repeated half ahead, sir.'

After that the orders went down thick and fast as Cameron manoeuvred the corvette up to the Japanese, whose decks were bloody with strips of flesh hanging from standing rigging and the remnants of the bridge and gun. The bridge wreckage, leaning further over to port now, seemed filled with bodies. Aboard the corvette the First Lieutenant, who had reported to the bridge as soon as the boarding orders had been passed, was standing by to jump the gap, a revolver in one hand, his full-dress sword in the other, his face set hard. Like CPO Rodman, he was reacting to the thrill of an old-fashioned boarding and like Rodman was seeing the Nelson touch, the individual, hand-to-hand fighting which seldom came the Navy's way.

Briar came up alongside and Cameron put his engine astern to check the way. As the ships came together, touching lightly so that there was only a faint jar, Cameron roared out through a megaphone, 'Boarding-party away!'

Frome was in the lead, the first across the gap. He saw a blur of yellow faces as the Japanese mustered to repel boarders, then they were all across and fighting hard for their lives. On the bridge Cameron's fists were balled, nails digging into his palms. He could have miscalculated; there was always a risk in boarding, the tables could be turned and a fighting mob of Japanese could spill over on to his own decks. At the moment Frome didn't seem to be having it his way; the Japanese were no cowards and the British seamen were hard pressed. Cameron sweated; he should have used the 4-inch and blasted the Jap from the water. Now he was powerless to use his guns; even the close-range weapons couldn't make distinctions if they were ordered to sweep the decks.

He saw the First Lieutenant go down, pouring blood from a head wound. He saw Lamprey giving Frome cover, standing over him and firing a revolver point-blank into some Japanese who were moving in to attack. Now there was no effective officer to lead the boarding-party. Cameron knew he couldn't keep out of it; he had to follow his instinct, the itch to take a personal part.

He said, 'Take over, Pilot.'

'You're not –'

Cameron didn't wait to hear the rest of it. He went down the bridge ladder fast and jumped the gap. This was wider now; he only just made it, landing in a heap on the Japanese fo'c'sle. Picking himself up, he bent again and seized a rifle from a man lying dead on the deck. He charged right through the Japanese seamen, firing a full clip of cartridges, working the bolt like a lunatic, then laying about with the bayonet as he turned back on them from their rear. He had a moment to see that Frome was alive, being assisted by Lamprey to sit up. A cheer went up from the British party when they saw the skipper was there in person; that seemed to give them a fresh spurt. Petty Officer Tebbs rushed headlong at an unusually tall Japanese who was about to strike at Lamprey, and butted him in the stomach with a head like a bullet. The man doubled and staggered backwards, fetching up against the bayonet of a British rating who had chosen a fortunate moment to swing round. There was a scream, and the tip of the bayonet, savagely lunged, came through the man's side and was withdrawn as he fell to the blood-slippery deck. Gradually now the Japanese seamen were being herded towards the fo'c'sle and the mangled remains of the gun and its crew.

Cameron shouted for his own ratings to keep off the fo'c'sle and hold the line just abaft the bridge. Then he called across to his own deck. It was Stripey Fish who answered.

'Get the close-range weapons lined up on the Japs,' Cameron shouted.

'Aye, aye, sir. Turn the buggers into yuman sieves, sir?'

'No! Not unless I give the order, Fish. Move!'

'Yessir!' Fish moved, very fast for his bulk, very much faster than was normal for him. On the bridge, Morgan put the engine a touch ahead to bring the port-side Oerlikon a little closer to the Japanese fo'c'sle, at the same time passing the action information to Parbutt in the engine-room. Parbutt was as tense as anyone, knowing the risks that Cameron had taken and half expecting to find yellow faces peering down any moment through the maze of pipes. He gave an expert touch ahead to his engine and waited for what might come next. He wiped sweat from his face with a handful of oily cotton-waste that left him looking like a streaky Negro. But it ought to be okay now from what Morgan had said. He wished he was up there on deck, behind the guns – he'd give the little buggers what for! It had been the Japs who'd sunk the old *Repulse* and the *Prince of Wales* in the South China Sea . . . .

Up top, Stripey Fish stared down at the Japs on their fo'c'sle; the Japs stared back, slap into the depressed muzzle of the Oerlikon. Fish's face was a big, happy smile: talk about power, the power of life and death if only the skipper would give the word. His finger hovered, all set to fire. The faces didn't look scared, just surly, but one blast and that would change. Fish heard Cameron's voice:

'If anyone speaks English, he can just pass the word around that I'm ready to open fire. I'm asking for surrender.'

He waited. English was hardly necessary; the close-range weapons were speaking very loudly for themselves. Still surly, the Japanese dropped their rifles. The First Lieutenant, recovered now but grim-faced, joined Cameron.

'Move in, sir?'

Cameron nodded. Frome passed the order and the hands went for'ard behind the rifles and bayonets. From their rear a head emerged from a hatch, and a hand came up clutching a rifle. There was a shout from Fish, and Lamprey turned in a flash and fired his revolver. The head jerked backwards and the top of the skull lifted. The rifle clattered on the deck and Lamprey turned away again, going with the others to take over the prisoners. There was no further trouble, and Stripey Fish was left with an unfulfilled feeling. Well, you couldn't expect the chance of a bull's-eye every time, he thought. He would have to go on living on the thrill of having shot down that aircraft.

'Smack it about, lads,' Gates said, sounding sharp. The sapper Major was looking impatiently around and there was tight forbearance showing on the face of Staff Sergeant Strong: seamen were all right afloat, bloody useless ashore. Sykes was dithering and the hands were making a cock of getting the army equipment into the inflatable dinghies for the second water-crossing. It had been a long, hard slog from where they'd been landed from the corvette ; the ground had been diabolical, mountains had had to be skirted, rocky outcroppings negotiated, and seamen were' unused to such antics. They were a sight wearier, Gates saw, than the soldiers, but he wasn't having them letting down the ship in full view of a load of brown jobs. 'Some of you, you're as much use as my Aunt Fanny's – '

He broke off; Sykes was calling him. 'Yes, sir ?'

'We'll have to get a move on.' Sykes had extricated his wrist from the sleeve of his duffel coat and was pointing at his watch. 'Time's getting short, you know.'

Yes, isn't it, you daft twat, Gates thought to himself, and if you'd put a bit of guts into it yourself the lads would have done better. Aloud he said, 'Doing their best, sir.'

'Well, they'd better,' Sykes said with a touch of petulance. Gates believed Sykes had had a chivvying from Dixon, who was a different kettle of fish, tenacious, hard as nails. Gates got in amongst the hands, working with them himself in the interest of speed, and they got the dinghies loaded. The first instalment set off across the water, heading for the island that was to be the first explosion site. Once ashore again, they would face another longish clamber over the horrible terrain. With the first batch went Major Dixon with Leading Seaman Hoggett ; Gates and Sykes stayed behind with Staff Sergeant Strong, waiting for the dinghies to come back and be loaded up again. Strong approached Sykes and gave a swinging salute.

'Sir !'

'Yes ?' Sykes fidgeted under the direct stare from Strong's eyes.

'With respect sir. We're a little open to view if any aircraft come over, sir.'

'Well, yes. But so are the dinghies, Sergeant.'

'That's inevitable, sir. But if they get attacked, the rest of us can still function so long as we're not dead. I suggest we get into cover.' Strong waved a hand around; there was cover of a sort, the lee of a hillside, some deep clefts in the level ground and some rocky outcrops. 'See what I mean, sir, do you ?'

Sykes nodded. 'Yes. All right, then. See to your men.' He called out again, 'Petty Officer Gates, we'd better have the hands in cover.'

'Aye, aye, sir.' Gates was discomfited – another one up to the army. Should have thought of it himself, and so should Mr Sykes. No excuse. Self-condemnation lent extra sharpness to his voice as he passed the orders and went around seeing that they were obeyed. His eye was as sharp as his voice. 'Beaner !'

'Yes, PO ?'

'Shove your backside in, we don't want the pleasure of seeing it nor do the Japs. *Move !*'

Beaner moved a fraction, withdrawing his offending rear from sight. He didn't like Gates ; Gates was always on to him, do this, do that. Not fair ; he hadn't wanted to join and so long as he did his work, his enforced work, for King and Country he didn't see why he should look keen about it.

Himself, he was keen on the one thing only and there was none of that available in perishing Tierre del Fuego or wherever it was. Withdrawn into cover but not comfort, Ordinary Seaman Beaner brooded until the dinghies came back across the water and he was ordered out again. No aircraft; that was something. If only they would keep off for long enough, he might yet get back to the ship again, and the messdecks were at least better than this. The ship gave you a safe feeling like the Bank of England, compared with this lot.

Two more trips across; when the whole party with all the gear was on the island, Dixon gave them the final briefing, aided by a large-scale map. 'There's where we lay the first set of charges – right on the northerly tip, where the island forms a peninsula jutting out towards the mainland. That's the narrowest part of the sea passage – right?'

Sykes nodded. 'Shallow too, of course.'

'Yes. That's the whole point and we can only hope it's a valid one. What we aim to do is to bring down the mountainside, slap into the water at that narrowest and shallowest part. Now, then.' Dixon's finger travelled west along the map. 'Here's where the second lot of charges will have to go, the ones that'll shut the Japs in at their rear. It means another sea trip and it'll have to be made bloody fast.' The spot chosen was some three miles from the first position across another stretch of water that was unnavigable to anything much bigger than a ship's boat. 'As soon as we've laid the first lot, we shift – and we just hope we get there before the Japs do. Setting the charges will take time, and it's impossible to estimate just how much time – at this moment, anyway. Once I've seen for myself how the first lot goes, then I'll be able to make some sort of estimate. Not that it'll help much if we get beaten to it – and we've no means of knowing how far off those ships are.' He paused. 'Any questions?'

'Yes,' Sykes said, pulling at his chin. 'Do I take it you blow the first lot, the eastern charges, right away? Or wait for the

Japanese to move in and hope to blow some of the ships up as well ?'

'The latter,' Dixon said. 'If you think about it, it's obvious. The sound of the explosion would only scare 'em off, right ? We *must* wait till they're in the narrows – or rather, just moving into them. All right ?'

Sykes said, 'Yes. But what about the second lot, Major ?'

'What about it ?'

'Do we wait till they're in before we blow ... same as the first lot ?'

Dixon stared at him. Gates, who was standing alongside Sykes, almost blew a gasket from sheer embarrassment for the Navy. Patiently Dixon said, 'Yes. Oh, yes. Because by that time they'll bloody well be in already, won't they ?'

'I meant – '

'All right, all right. Just leave it.' Dixon laid a hand on Sykes' shoulder. 'What I intend to do is to leave two men behind to blow the first lot, and just as soon as we hear the result, we blow the second lot. It'll be almost simultaneous, you see. Then we've got them.' He looked around at the waiting men. 'Right ! Let's move out.'

They set to and humped the gear onwards ; the weather was worsening, deadly cold and starting to blow again. There was a flurry of snow and within a few minutes the stuff was coming down thick and fast, a real blizzard. Sykes found he could hardly see a thing, that it was sheer agony to keep his eyes open. He stumbled on ; the party had a boat's compass with them but Sykes rapidly became too numb in mind and body to make proper use of it, and Dixon took over, using his pocket compass. Sykes trudged on behind him, stumbling, falling, being heaved to his feet by Gates, now acting as officer's prop. Sykes began to believe he was done for, that none of them could survive.

He said as much in a high voice to Gates.

'Don't you believe it,' Gates said. He told a white lie. 'I've known worse. Besides, if we can't see where we are, neither can the Japs – can't find us, I mean. There's always a silver bloody lining. Watch your step now, sir – whoops-a-daisy, my, aren't we being bloody clumsy!' Once more he hoisted Sykes back on to his feet. The wind moaned eerily, sent the snow biting into any exposed bit of flesh, not that there was much of that about Mr Sykes who couldn't see largely because he had his duffel-coat hood right over his face and a thick woollen muffler up to his eyes and beyond. *Roll on the Nelson, the Rodney, Renown,* Gates thought, *this muffled-up bastard is getting me down* . . .

The Japanese vessel was named the *Oishi*; her First Lieutenant was alive and not badly injured: a shot-up shoulder, where a rifle bullet had passed through a fleshy overhang beneath the arm-pit. Cameron got the SBA to check it over and bandage it, then he had the Japanese officer brought to the bridge for questioning. The man had quite good English.

Cameron said, 'I want to know the disposition of your ships in the vicinity.'

'No. I say nothing – name and rank only. Geneva Convention.'

'Which you stick to rigidly, of course.'

'Yes. International Law –'

'As you do in the case of our prisoners-of-war?'

'Not comment.'

Cameron gave a hard laugh. 'You don't surprise me! But you're going to talk about your ships out here.'

'Not talk.'

Cameron stared the officer in the eyes. They remained steady, no flicker of fear of what might happen to him. Cameron had some knowledge of the Japanese willingness to die for their Emperor. He would probably get nowhere and was not prepared to go to the extreme length of physical pressure which probably wouldn't work in any case. There were other avenues and currently Frome, together with the leading telegraphist, was ransacking the enemy warship's

96

W/T office and the signal files for anything that might prove helpful. True, it would all be in Japanese characters and none of his ship's company would understand a word; but the prisoners were not going to be sure of that and there was a possible pressure point if only he could find the right approach. He said, 'I believe you'll talk soon. If you don't, one of your men will.'

'In Japanese . . . if talk at all.' There was a wide smile; Cameron ignored it and nodded at the coxswain, who was standing behind the prisoner with an armed escort of two ratings. The Japanese officer was removed below, where the ship was now badly overcrowded again, this time with the prisoners-of-war instead of the sappers. They had been crammed into the space just aft of the seamen's messdeck, under a strong guard, and they were squatting and staring impassively in front of them, exuding an air of confidence that before long they would be freed. The leading seaman in charge of the guard, by name Blanchard, could sense this.

'Just like they knew,' he said to Lamprey when the buffer came in to check security.

'Knew what?'

'Well, that some of their ships are coming in, the big stuff. I 'ope the skipper 'as some luck, making some of 'em talk.'

'He won't. You know what these buggers are like.'

'I dunno,' Blanchard said reflectively. 'They're no more'n human. A bayonet up the arse could work miracles.'

'Don't you try it,' Lamprey said 'We're *British*.' He went on his way, leaving Blanchard to rub at his nose and narrow his eyes at the squatting Japs. British my arse, Blanchard was thinking, this war's killing that sort of sentiment stone dead. This war had to be won, full stop. Didn't matter how. Give the Japs a taste of their own medicine, that was the thing. If the officers wouldn't do it, well, maybe someone else could. But Blanchard hadn't an idea in the world as to how. Not at the moment. Something might come into his head; he wasn't daft and in his younger days he'd had to watch out for himself since no one else did. His childhood had been hard. His old man was always on the bottle and always on his old lady too – the Blanchards were a large family as a result, more of them than there were Fishes in fact. One day his old man had come home more boozed than usual and had fallen down the stairs and broken his neck. After that the old lady had gone to pieces. She'd ended up in a loony bin and the family had been shoved into an orphanage, a situation from which Blanchard had constantly run away, which only made matters worse after he was brought back, but he managed to live on his wits while at liberty – his wits and his fists. He had become cunning and as tough as a boot; and he'd joined the Navy as soon as he'd been old enough, a seaman boy in the stone frigate *St Vincent* at Gosport.

That, too, had been hard, though in a different way. Boy Second Class Blanchard had had to fight his way up the ladder, live down his past, and live down some service misdemeanours as well, to get his eventual rate. Having got it, he'd lost it again and done some time in Detention Quarters at Pompey; then, after a long interval, he'd got it back. But while in the Navy's version of Dartmoor he'd learned another thing or two.

Bollocks to the velvet glove, it didn't get anybody anywhere.

Surveying the Jap faces, his mind got busy. He reckoned he could do the skipper and all of them a good turn. It would be chancing his arm again if things went wrong, but no good worrying about that. Faint heart never won fair lady or anything else in this life.

'Hup-hup-hup,' Gates called out. 'Lift your rotten feet over the snow, for Christ's sake.' The blizzard had ceased but the fallen snow was thick as Sykes. Sykes was better now; he'd cleared a way for his face, and he was still moving. Not exactly leading; Gates was doing that. Conferring with Major Dixon, Gates established that the target area was now only around half a mile ahead ; and there was no sign of any Jap activity either in the air or on the water. Gradually as the visibility cleared the mountains came up again, stark, grim and snow-covered. There was still a wind and it was still bitter, enough to freeze the bone-marrow. God, what a place ! the Japs had to be barmy, just to even think of coming through this way. Plunging on through the snow, Gates thought again about that ghostly ship that had passed them out at sea.

What had she been after ? And who was she ?

No answer to that for now, but Gates had a hunch it could be relevant enough. Word had filtered down through the ship just after, that the skipper believed they could have been outflanked, that an attack had already been mounted on the Falklands. If so, what were they all doing here ? Surely some-one would have sent a signal calling the whole show off, or didn't they give a hoot for the poor little *Briar* ?

Likely enough, was that. Gates gave a hollow laugh.

'What's up ?' Sykes asked, right behind him where the officer shouldn't be.

Gates said, 'Thoughts. That's all. Not worth a penny, even if you was to make the offer.' His voice grated ; his throat was hoarse from doing Sykes' job for him – encouraging beyond the duties of a non-commissioned ramrod. There were plenty of times, and this was one, where an officer's stripes were of more value than the crossed anchors of a PO. Junior ratings, until they learned different, believed the sun shone out of an officer's backside because it was the wardroom officers who knew the facts and whose word of reassurance held weight.

But never mind. There were plenty of good officers and that Dixon was one. If anyone could pull them through this, he would. And the skipper, back aboard the ship, wouldn't let them down either.

There was a call from ahead and a moment later Gates saw Staff Sergeant Strong coming back towards the Naval party.

'Water ahead,' Strong called out. 'We're there, or just about. First lot of charges.'

Sykes waved a hand; he seemed beyond speech now, puffing like a grampus under his topweight of wool. They moved on, taking it faster now the target was in sight. The hands began to overtake Sykes. Sykes didn't give a damn. His feet hurt and he felt sick and once again there was a flurry of snow starting from the west, whirling along the wind. Let Gates do the shepherding, that was what he was there for. Sykes felt a cold fury that he'd been sent along at all. All that sea watchkeeping, and now this. No one would have stood for it back in peacetime ... eighteen hours a day plus! War or not, they were still only human, still had their rights, still needed their rest. He used to think it was pretty hard graft at Woolworth's at times, stocktaking for instance when he didn't get home till gone ten. He hadn't appreciated his luck.

There was another shout from ahead and Dixon appeared over some rising ground at the foot of a sheer mountainside; he was coming back at the double with his sappers.

He saw Sykes labouring along behind the seamen.

'Cover!' he called out. 'Bloody fast!' He ran on, coming down the slope.

'What's up?' Sykes asked, eyes wide.

Dixon reached him. 'Ship. Looks like a smallish Jap cruiser, entering from the east – not the west, mark you. We won't have been seen, but this is a time for lying low.'

9

'MUST have bin doing a recce,' Gates said. 'When she passed us at sea. Now she's on her way back to rejoin.' He paused; Sykes hadn't ticked over. 'That ghost ship!'

'How do we know it's the same one?' Sykes asked.

'We don't,' Gates answered briefly. 'It's an assumption, sir, that's all. But I reckon it's a fair enough one.' He gave a shiver; the cold was getting worse with their current inaction, holed up in one of the clefts in the hard rock. 'Just a general recce of the sea area between the Falklands and the Le Maire Strait.'

'Well, perhaps. We just don't know. The thing is, what do we do now?'

Gates said, 'I reckon we ought to make contact with the skipper, sir. Let him know.'

'Go back aboard?' Hope had leaped into Sykes' voice.

Gates said, 'No, sir. Send the bunting tosser to raise the skipper. That's why we brought him. Use his Aldis soon as he has the ship in VS range. All right?'

Sykes dithered. What – if he had been present – would the Captain have done? There was nothing Sykes wished for more than to get back to the corvette but it was his duty to remain with the party and, probably, carry on as before once the Japanese cruiser had passed on out of sight. He said, 'Basically, the situation doesn't really seem to have changed, does it?'

It was Dixon who answered, a look of growing impatience on his face. 'No, it hasn't. My chaps will be going in once that ship's gone. But I agree with your PO. Your Captain should be informed – pronto.' He met Gates' eye ; the expression of both men remained unchanged, but a good deal of understanding passed between them. 'You'd better get on with it. If you – ' He broke off; the Naval rating left to spot the passage of the cruiser from a covered vantage point had got to his feet and was coming down the slope towards them. 'Well ?'

'Passed out of sight, sir,' Beaner reported. 'And it was a cruiser all right, a light cruiser, I reckon.'

Gates didn't wait for Sykes. He nodded and raised his voice. 'Bunts ?'

The signalman looked up. Gates said, 'Officer wants you, make VS contact with the ship.' He glanced at Sykes. 'Best give him a couple of hands,' he said. 'This weather . . . not the time and place to be on your own. Better take the boat's compass an' all.' He got to his feet, detailed two seamen and mustered the rest. The explosives were taken up again and Dixon led the main party back towards the long finger of the peninsula.

There was no room for a decent pacing of the bridge and the cold was appalling. Cameron went down to the upper deck and walked fore and aft, beating his arms around his body. He wouldn't go below ; anything could happen at any moment. The absence of air activity was welcome yet at the same time disquieting. That one aircraft had been shot down and the loss must be known by now ; and there was the question of the disabled *Oishi*, whose absence might also be noted soon. Cameron had grappled her alongside his own vessel, with ropes made fast to the bitts on either ship, to prevent her drifting across the entry to the inlet and being spotted by the enemy or the neutrals whose waters they were in. The damage to her fo'c'sle had precluded any possibility of anchoring her, and in any case the water was very deep where they lay and she wouldn't have got enough cable on the bottom to hold her if the wind increased.

No progress had been made with the Japanese seamen or their First Lieutenant. By this time the contents of the ship's signal file and the code books in the W/T office had been brought across – no help there either. Japanese was Japanese. But below, outside the seamen's messdeck, Blanchard, unknown to Cameron, was working on his own interpretation of interrogation. In Blanchard's view, fear was the thing that opened mouths wide. Fear had been part of his own childhood – fear of his old man, fear of the matron in the orphanage, fear of the cops when he was on the run from the home. Blanchard knew the effects of fear. He picked out the Jap he considered most likely, not necessarily to react quickly to fear, but to speak English.

This man had what Blanchard would have called a profess-orial look about him – learned, clerkly, huge spectacles and a rather cissy manner. There was nothing of the seaman about him ; maybe he wasn't a seaman, Blanchard had no knowledge of the Japs' naval badges, he could have been a cook, a poultice walloper or a po bosun, perhaps. Anyway, the general impression was of a Japanese gent who'd been conscripted to serve with a load of serfs and didn't go much on his companions. Toffee-nosed was what he looked.

Leading Seaman Blanchard began to talk big to the ratings of the POW guard. A lot of guff about what could be done with prisoners : feed the bastards into the boilers, drop them over the side with weights attached, force bayonets into their mouths, ears, eyes . . . anywhere else you cared to dream up. Carve up their stomachs like they did with their own hari-kiri. As he yacked away, he watched the gent Jap from the corner of an eye. The little yellow bugger was turning green, eyes wide, listening intently to it all. He would have been told by his officers and the politicians that the British were barbarians who would stop at nothing. He was nicely prepared ground.

And he played right into Blanchard's hands.

He stood up and said in English, 'Please.'

'So you speak English, eh?'

'Yes. Please.'

He didn't add anything to that but he was squirming about ... squirming and being squeamish. Blanchard, understanding that this was a case of the runs, grinned and said, 'Want to go to the 'eads, is that it?'

'Please ... '

'All right then, me Jap boyo, you shall.' Blanchard turned to the armed British ratings on guard. 'You lot stay 'ere. *I'll* take him. Come on, you,' he said to the Japanese. The man picked his way daintily past his squatting shipmates and was taken over by Blanchard, who thrust his bayonetted rifle into his back and propelled him over a coaming after unclipping a watertight door. Closing the door behind him, he pushed the prisoner onward and into the seamen's heads.

Blanchard filled the entrance with his heavy body, keeping his rifle aimed at the Japanese, who was now looking very full of fear.

'Now,' Blanchard said. 'Just you an' me, right?' He unfastened his bayonet and moved towards the Jap with it in his hand. His eyes were hard and his mouth, above a firm chin, was a thin, bloodless line. The Jap cringed and uttered a yelp.

'Shut up,' Blanchard said. Blanchard was thinking: poor little sod, on his own he mightn't ever hurt a fly, he'd just been caught up in it like they all had, but he was a weak link and he had to suffer in the Allied interest ....

Ten minutes later Leading Seaman Blanchard emerged on to the upper deck with the Jap, whose name he now knew was Toshio Sato, steward aboard the *Oishi*, wide-eyed in front of the Lee Enfield rifle and shaking badly. Meeting Cameron on deck, Blanchard addressed him.

'Beg pardon, sir – '

'Yes?'

'This person, this Jap, sir. Speaks English, sir. Thought I'd report it, like.'

Cameron nodded. 'Could be useful, Blanchard.'

'*Will* be, sir! I guarantee that, sir. I 'eard about codes an' such. 'E'll interpret, sir.'

'How do you know?'

''E said so, sir.' Blanchard smirked.

Cameron raised an eyebrow. 'He did, did he? How come? How did you manage it?'

Blanchard said off-handedly, 'Bit o' bullshit, sir, that's all.'

Cameron gave him a hard stare, searching the granite face. 'I hope you didn't overstep the mark, Blanchard. No rough stuff?'

'What, me, sir?' Blanchard was genuinely indignant. 'Course not, sir! I wouldn't do anything like that. Gentle as a lamb, sir. Give you me word, sir, it was all done by what you might call persuasion.' Blanchard moved closer and hissed into Cameron's ear. 'I told 'im you an' the First Lootenant, sir, were a right paii, a couple o' bleedin' bastards ... 'ope you don't mind, sir.'

'Blanchard did a first-class job, sir,' Frome said. Cameron agreed. Toshio Sato – and Blanchard had been right about his civilian status: he had been a schoolmaster – had interpreted to good effect. It was all there; the Admiralty's original suspicions stood confirmed in the plain-language versions of coded signals. The Japanese were mounting an assault against the lightly-held British base in the Falklands, intending to land troops on the inhospitable coast of West Falkland, consolidate there and then move from a position of strength to take East Falkland and establish their own base at Port Stanley from where they would be in a good position to harass the convoys moving around the Cape of Good Hope. Confirmed also was the Admiralty's belief that the Japanese were present in greater strength than had initially been suspected: detailed for the assault and currently in the waters north of Cape Horn were three heavy cruisers – the *Ichikawa* wearing the flag of Rear-Admiral Yamanaka, the *Sasebo* and the *Hakodate* escorting a flotilla of big seagoing tank landing craft; and a fleet aircraft-carrier was currently standing off the western entry to the Magellan Strait, held in reserve until a landing had been made when she would move in at speed around Cape Horn to bring her fighter aircraft to bear in support.

'That's where those aircraft came from,' Frome said.

Cameron wasn't listening; he looked out across the water of the inlet; the visibility was down again – more snow. He blew out his breath, tapped the scrawled translation notes which he had laid on the chart table. The Japanese commander had indicated his expected time schedule in his signals to the *Oishi*. 'Doesn't give us long,' Cameron said to Morgan. 'Two hours after nightfall, they'll be in the narrows.' He looked at the clock in the fore part of the bridge. 'Dark in what – six hours.'

'Plus a bit,' Morgan said. 'Seven hours, sir.'

'In this muck?'

'No, not if it keeps up.'

Cameron said, 'I'm reckoning on six. Eight hours all told . . . and not a bloody word from the landing-party.'

'They'll be having a tough job, sir,' Frome said in another oblique reference to the weather. He gave an edgy laugh. 'D'you know, I'm just beginning to think we've been landed with more than we can chew!'

Cameron nodded. 'I've been thinking that for quite a while, Number One – but we're going to bloody well eat it all the same.'

The snow was falling relentlessly now. It had begun about half an hour after Signalman Thurgood had started back for the ship with Quinn and Able Seaman Denton, light at first then a real blizzard. The entire land stood white, the water

106

between was dully metallic. The going was immensely slow and became slower ; even the blood seemed to reach freezing point as the three men battered their onward way through appalling visibility.

'Not all that far,' Thurgood said. His teeth chattered, set in a blue face.

Quinn said, 'They'll never read the Aldis.'

'Maybe they won't. If they can't, we'll have to try to swim across ourselves. Or one of us will.'

That, Quinn thought, was a daft suggestion . . . . Ordinary Seaman Quinn was learning fast that the Navy wasn't all battleships steaming grandly out of Portsmouth harbour, *Rule*, *Britannia* on the brass, and chief gunners' mates bawling their lungs out on the parade at the Royal Naval Barracks. Different here . . . for one thing it was almost totally silent – would have been one hundred per cent if it hadn't been for the wind over the hilltops, wind that came down all too often through the dips in the range to smash the snow into their faces. Captain Scott had been a hero right enough ! Quinn struggled on and after some more progress he heard an oath, followed by a cry of pain that ended very suddenly in a nasty, strangulated sound.

Pressing ahead, face anxious beneath the snow, he all but fell over something.

A body, it was. Thurgood's. And there was blood. Hoarsely Quinn shouted at him. 'What's up, mate ? All right, are you ?'

There was no answer. Denton was alongside him now, and bending. Denton said, 'Christ, he's a goner. Look !'

Quinn looked, and saw somthing horrible. Thurgood had tripped and fallen and in falling a sharp sliver of upthrust rock had gone clean through his muffler and duffel-coat hood and into his neck. The snow was becoming more blood-stained every moment and Thurgood was as dead as a doornail.

'Bloody hell,' Quinn said softly. 'What do we do, eh ?'

'Leave him. Then go on. All we can do.'

'Doesn't seem right.'

'I know. Sod the bloody war. Look, we can't bury him, that's obvious. He'll keep – it's like a fridge. We can come back for him.'

Quinn knew that was daft, there simply wouldn't be time. As soon as the job was done the skipper would piss off out, back by way of Cape Horn. But Quinn didn't say so ; Denton had meant to be comforting. By the time they were on the move again the snow had already almost obliterated Thurgood's body and it didn't seem so bad leaving him ; it was like a kind of burial. You always had to leave after that.

Quinn found himself getting weird ideas. Hallucinations . . . he could see Palmerston Road in Southsea before the Blitz wiped it out. Handley's on the corner of Portland Road, the Westminster Bank right opposite on the Osborne Road corner. Bright's, Morant's, Boots, W.H. Smith. His mother walking past the Mikado Café, down towards St Jude's Church – which in fact was still there. There was a curious drumming in his ears and he was getting sleepy and, oddly, it didn't seem so cold. Portsmouth Hard . . . he was bicycling towards the Hard, past the *Vernon* torpedo school and under the railway bridge that carried the track from the harbour station to Waterloo. Across St George's Square was the local NAAFI head office. NAAFI with its ships' canteens, bars of nutty, fags and soft drinks.

He could do with some of that . . .

Quinn was totally unaware that he was no longer moving, that he was lying in a heap, unnoticed by Denton who had been in the lead. By the time the AB had ticked over, Quinn had vanished in the snow behind. Denton felt the onset of panic. He went back a few paces, then stopped. What was the point ? He could miss Quinn by a mile. He turned back, followed the dictates of the boat's compass. That was all they'd had to go on for some while now ; so little was visible through the appalling blizzard. Just follow the bearing.

Denton stumbled on, determined to reach the ship. He was bloody nearly frozen; his breath cracked before his face, freezing as it left his mouth. He couldn't feel his feet; it was like walking on a cloud.

When he fell into the snow-filled cleft that he was unable to see, he lay spread-eagled, as numb and useless as a beetle that had landed in marmalade. All desire to move left him.

10

THE snow was spread over the whole area running north from Cape Horn, right through to Punta Arenas. It was affecting everybody: the Japanese cruisers and landing-craft, ready to move eastwards towards the Falklands, were held in the channels and side inlets; the navigation was tricky at the best of times, and now it was impossible. In Punta Arenas the neutral Chilean warships remained under their snow blanket, unable to move out on patrol. On *Briar's* bridge, Cameron stood like a snowman, knowing that no further decisions could be reached until the blizzard passed.

Behind him another snowman tramped his feet up and down and flailed his arms: Morgan, to whom all this was the farest of cries from the mostly fair-weather Orient run. Morgan was wondering what the hell they were doing up there on the bridge and he was about to say so when Cameron turned round.

'It's going to last, Pilot.'

'Yes, sir.'

'Total inhibition of air activity. You'd better get below.'

'What about you?' Morgan asked.

'I'll stay. If necessary, Number One can relieve decks. Off you go, Pilot.'

Morgan went, thankfully enough. Cameron dismissed one of the lookouts. 'One of you is enough till this lot passes over,' he said. 'Tell the buffer I want fifteen-minute spells organized,' he added to the man who was going off watch.

Sending the leading signalman below, he remained in the fore part of the bridge, alone but for one lookout. Head sunk in his arms, he tried to work out the next move. So many enemy ships . . . a lot to block in, but not impossible. He had been about to send hands ashore with a message for the sappers when the snow had started and he knew that any such mission would be hopeless. Dixon had yet to be warned of the fresh intelligence ; on the other hand the warning might not be necessary. Dixon would see the ships for himself in due course and would probably have set the charges widely enough apart in any case – he'd had that earlier warning from the Admiralty that the presence of more ships had been suspected.

In a sense the snow was helping them. Dixon would have more time before the Japs moved through – bound to ; no one would risk movement yet. So far, so good, always provided the sappers weren't coming up against difficulties apart from the snow. The laying of charges in rock was always problematical. Cameron's personal worry was what he should do when the blizzard stopped. Wait where he was, wait for word from Dixon, or get under way towards the approaches to the Beagle Channel to be ready to embark the troops and his own landing-party ?

Hearing snow-muffled footsteps on the ladder, he turned. Frome had come up.

'Hullo there, Number One.'

'You all right, sir ?'

'As well as can be expected,' Cameron answered, grimacing through snow that had frozen round his lips. 'What's it like below ?'

'Nasty cold fug,' Frome said. 'Very smelly !'

'I won't ask if the lower deck's in good spirits. Talking of which, I fancy an extra rum issue would be welcome. What d'you think ?'

'It would be very much appreciated, sir.'

'Make it, then. Get the LSA off his bottom.'

'Aye, aye, sir. What about the T men ?'

'What about them ?'

'Well, mostly they're only T because of the threepence a day in lieu. There aren't many genuine teetotallers – '

'And they feel the cold just as much as the grog men! All right, Number One, I'll take it on my own head – exigencies of the Service – and take any rockets that come from the cox'n for buggering up his books.'

Frome went below. There was another category in the rum issue : UA, or Under Age ... every rating in the fleet was either T for Temperance, G for Grog, or UA. UA ratings also felt the cold and no doubt had a drink when ashore. But to authorize rum aboard for anyone under twenty would bring down thunder and lightning plus the Board of Admiralty. However, Cameron covered this. Before the First Lieutenant had reached the upper deck, he was called back.

'The UA men, Number One. Give them a tot of whisky each from my own stock. That way, we keep the record straight.'

Grinning, Frome went down the ladder again. When the issue was made, there was plenty of comment about the skipper. For a Captain, he was almost human. As Stripey Fish remarked, anyone who poured booze into a matloe was a good bloke.

The snow hadn't stopped Dixon. By the time it had come on enough to be a hindrance the sappers had reached the first target area and the positions for the charges had been marked out. Thereafter Staff Sergeant Strong and Dixon himself got cracking with the rest and never mind the conditions. It was a job for concentrated minds and the concentration helped them to disregard the cold as the picks got busy digging out the holes for the explosive, a nice wide spread that if all went well would bring down ton after ton of the mountainside to cascade into the narrow channel. And when the Jap ships had been brought up all standing there would still be a nice load of rock dropping down on their decks. Dixon believed the leading ship would go hard aground, though not so the ones behind – they were the ones that would need the blocking-in astern.

Petty Officer Gates also believed the grounding theory. He spoke of it to Sykes while the Naval party, whose job was done for the time being, kept in such cover as they could find in the lee of an outcrop of rock close to the water, a place where a small overhang gave some, but not much, shelter from the falling snow. Sykes was wedged right at the inward end of the overhang, sunk into his woollen cocoon. Like a chrysalis, Gates thought.

Sykes asked, 'Won't its speed carry it through?'

'No, sir. Because the sappers'll blow the lot at the right time, which is just before she comes abeam like.' He added, 'Not likely to be going that fast anyway, is she?'

'Oh.' Sykes nodded. 'God, it's cold!'

'Take some exercise,' Gates suggested. 'Do a few press-ups.' He laughed, thinking of the spectacle *that* would be, all that wool on the down-and-up.

'It's not funny, Gates.'

'No, it's not.' Gates looked at him; it was pathetic rather than funny. Gates had a son, nine years old. Ronnie would probably follow him into the Andrew – he'd already shown a lot of interest and from the age of five had gone mad with excitement during the pre-war Navy Weeks in the dockyard. He was more of a man at nine than this streak of piss. If Gates had had a son like Mr Sykes, he'd have kicked his arse all the way from Nelson's *Victory*, out through the Main Gate of the yard, down Queen Street, along Commercial Road to Portsdown Hill, a nice long way. Gates thought about his father, also a Navy man, who'd made warrant rank as boatswain before the last lot and then had gone down at Jutland, serving aboard a cruiser. The old man had been a tough nut, all right – Gates didn't remember a lot about him, but he remembered that. Ronnie might well take after him and Gates looked forward to the day when the lad would be made upper yardman in line for a straight-stripe commission. Sub-Lieutenant Gates . . . it would be quite something.

Sykes broke into his thoughts. 'Do you think the sappers'll be much longer?'

'Couldn't say, sir. Getting tired, are you?'

'Well, yes – yes, I am. It's been a long stretch, with no time off since I was on watch.'

'Hard life, the Andrew.'

'I would never have chosen it myself, you know.' Sykes paused and came close to home and Gates' earlier thoughts. 'You a family man, Gates?'

'Yes.'

'Me, too. Being overseas like this . . . you miss the best days, when the kids are young.'

Gates said stonily, 'You've not been out from UK a dog-watch yet.'

'What?'

'You heard – sir. Me, I done a three-year commission in Hong Kong, and two up the straits – Med Fleet. Three and two away from home. Now, that's *absence*.' He gave a hard laugh. 'Some of you temporary officers, you don't know you're born yet.'

'There's no need to be impertinent,' Sykes said savagely.

Gates held on to his rising temper. 'I apologize.'

'You'd better.' Sykes sulked for a minute or so, then said, 'I think you'd better send a man to ask Major Dixon how long he's going to be.'

'In this?' Gates jerked a hand out into the blinding snow. 'Stumble into the water I shouldn't wonder. Talk about murder!'

'I –'

'Besides, Major Dixon knows *exactly* where we are. When he's ready, he'll come and say so. But that won't be before the snow stops and he can see where he's putting his feet.

114

He's taking a risk in laying the charges in this soup – sure he is – but no sane officer's going to take bleedin' *unnecessary* risks.' Gates paused. 'Of course, if you give the *order* –'

'That's enough, thank you,' Sykes snapped. He seethed inside, full now of self-pity. If he lost a man in spite of advice from his PO, it might come back on him afterwards.

Risking his life with every step he took, Dixon went round all the charge positions, checked them, checked the watertight fuse lines running to the firing box. The job was as well done as it could be. And he fancied the blizzard was easing off and about time too, though in point of fact it could have gone on for days. There was less bite and the visibility was just a shade better and improving. Fine – except for the one thing : soon the Japanese ships could be on their way through and there was work yet to be done. As soon as he could see his way, Dixon tramped through the snow to where the Naval party was sheltering.

'First lot of charges in place, Sykes. You look as if you've had a nice stand-easy, so we'll get on the move for the second lot pronto, all right ?'

Sykes had lurched to his feet, reaching out a hand to steady himself against the rock. 'I suppose so – yes.'

Petty Officer Gates asked, 'Fall the lads in, sir ?'

'Yes. What about informing the ship ?'

Gates said, 'I doubt if that's possible now, sir.'

'But the orders were that we should.'

'Yes, sir. I know the orders. But times change . . . that snow. All landmarks gone, no spare compass available now, it went with the bunting tosser if you remember, sir. So did the Aldis. No one'd never make it, not now.'

Sykes dithered. 'But . . . oh, all right. Just fall them in, then.'

'Aye, aye, sir.' Gates, glad to be on the move again and occupied in getting the job done, gestured the party to muster. The sappers brought their equipment in and the ratings once again took the strain as bearers. Dixon told Sykes that his Staff Sergeant would remain with six sappers to blow the charges, without further orders, as soon as the first enemy ship was in position below the peaks, by which time it would be up to the rest of them to have the second spread of charges laid and ready to fire.

The trek began again, short now of Thurgood, Denton and Quinn. Gates was doubtful if those three had ever made it. He was equally doubtful if any of them were going to get through; the going was terrible as they followed Dixon's pocket compass. Just a bloody great field of white, deep and treacherous, with rock jagging through here and there. Gates pushed on doggedly, his feet growing as heavy as lead after a while, moving ahead and back again along the line, doing Sykes' job for him again. Sykes had only himself in mind and was making the worst of it.

The progress was dead slow. It was going to take them too long. The weather had cleared amazingly. For Gates' money the Japs were going to seize their chance before it came down again, which it was bound to.

The change in the weather had brought some cheer to the corvette but it brought its anxieties as well: anxieties similar to Gates'.

'They'll be moving, Number One,' Cameron said. 'Any time now, and there's been nothing from Dixon's lot. The weather won't have been helping him.'

'We could send someone to make contact now the weather's – '

'No. They'd have a hell of a journey , Number One. The snow'll be feet deep and any wind'll mean heavy drifting. I doubt if it's a reasonable risk.'

'Wait for the sappers?'

'No. I'm moving out, Number One. I've a feeling something's gone wrong. I want to know what, and I want to be ready.' Cameron scanned the surrounding hills and water

116

through his binoculars. 'Pipe hands to stations, right away.'
He went to the engine-room voice-pipe. 'Chief?'

'Yessir!'

'I'll want your engines in two minutes. All ready?'

'Everything on top line, sir,' Parbutt said.

'Right! Stand by, then.'

'Stand by, sir.' The Chief ERA paused. 'Any gen, sir?'

'When there is,' Cameron answered, 'I'll let you know
right away. At the moment, we're just going out on a recce.'
He put back the voice-pipe cover. Below, Parbutt cast an eye
over his dials and gauges, noting readings almost
subconsciously, noting plenty of shine. Gleaming brasswork
– did it matter? Yes, it did. A clean, tiddley engine-room
was an efficient one. Slack off on that, and the hands slacked
off in other directions too. Parbutt wondered what the next
step might be, what sort of lark they would be steaming into
on the thrust and swirl of his engines. A moment later he
heard a clang along the ship's side. Not a bomb, nothing like
that, probably just the Jap being cast off and some unhandy
so-and-so of a seaman rating dropping gear about the place.
Any minute now, they would be under way; Parbutt was
watching the telegraph, ready to obey the instant the pointer
moved to Slow Ahead or Slow Astern. He wiped the back of
a hand across his lips. Talk about dry; and what he couldn't
do to a pint of Sam Smith's if he was back in West Auckland
and never mind that sister of his. Best forget about leave,
though, it wouldn't be on the cards for a dickens of a while
yet.

Parbutt found himself shaking a little. Funny thing about
the telegraph . . . it was always the same with him, each time
when the thing showed Stand By Main Engines after a period
of Finished With Engines, he got an attack of the jitters in
case he wasn't swift enough off the mark to put the steam
through when the pointer moved. Thereafter – no trouble.
Slow to Half to Full Away, easy. Just one of those things,
personal to himself.

117

On the bridge Cameron watched the *Oishi* drift away, denuded of her ship's company, wondered where she would fetch up. She might be a giveaway but he had no option – and it wouldn't be long before he was clear of the inlet and leaving it far behind. God alone knew what they might meet along the way, of course, and he would have no option about that either.

'Right, Pilot. Slow ahead, wheel fifteen to port.'

The order was repeated, acknowledged from below.

'Midships . . . steady.'

In the wheelhouse Chief Petty Officer Rodman let the wheel run through his hands, noted the course and reported it up the voice-pipe. *Briar* headed out of the inlet, back into the main channel. Cameron had laid off his course on the chart: he was heading right for the narrows, the first blow-up point, hoping eventually to pick up the landing-party somewhere in the vicinity. The weather remained clear as *Briar* went on at full speed, but the wind was increasing. Where that wind blew down the gullies the water was ruffled, with short, spume-topped waves. In the more sheltered parts the sea was flat enough – and the wind was welcome, keeping away the snow clouds until such time as it would gather more and send them in to bedevil navigation.

'What if we meet the Japs?' Morgan asked suddenly.

Cameron said, 'If we meet them we'll have to turn and run. David and Goliath . . . all very well but there's nothing to be gained that way. Pop-guns don't damage armoured ships, right?'

'Dead right, sir.'

Morgan's tone was flat. Down in the wheelhouse the coxswain had overheard the exchange and was looking thoughtful. None of them liked the idea of running away, but the skipper was right. No point in useless heroics that might jeopardize the whole operation. Often enough it took courage to run when you knew it was the only way and knew, too, that you would have to justify yourself to the Admiralty

118

afterwards. Rodman pulled out a packet of Gold Flake and lit a fag. He didn't go much on the Admiralty; they made their decisions and issued their judgments at leisure, not like commanding officers at sea. In Rodman's view officers were entitled to their undoubted privileges. Gold braid meant responsibility and the taking back of cans – so did his own crossed torpedoes, crown and wheel on his collar, but not in quite such measure. And good luck to the skipper. He had quite a job on hand . . . .

Cameron had; there were many things to consider, many decisions he could have made. The point about jeopardizing the operation was much in his mind. He could do that just by moving into the area if the Japanese timing had indeed altered, which it might have done if, say, they'd received weather reports to indicate that more snow was expected before their intended departure time. But would they have received anything? Probably not; they, too, were in land-locked waters where wireless reception would be next to impossible. On the other hand they might be getting help from the Chileans, possibly in more ways than just the pass-ing of weather information.

You had to be a bit of a politician as well as a seaman when you were in neutral waters. What were the relations between Chile and Japan, between Chile and the UK?

He ought to know, but he didn't.

Nor did Morgan or Frome. They hadn't a clue. Morgan was still mentally Australia-oriented, and Frome had no inter-est in the world's political set-up outside Hitler's Europe, while Cameron's briefing back in Port Stanley had indicated only the broad aspect of neutrality and the need to respect it so far as possible, which had been bunk in a sense because the mere fact of sending *Briar* in was a violation in itself. But the phrase *so far as possible* held significance when Cameron thought about it now. That could have many interpretations and any of them could be used later against a CO who'd made a cock of things. Down here it would be only too easy to do

119

that ; a lot of Tierra del Fuego and its contiguous seas belonged in fact to the Argentine ; plenty of wires could
become crossed.

Briar moved on ; by Morgan's reckoning, she would close
the narrows in a little over an hour. The sea route was a good
deal longer than the partly overland one taken by the
landing-party but *Briar* had the advantage of her speed.

Gates' assumption had been a good one : the Japanese light
cruiser *Sasebo* – she was little bigger than a destroyer – had
indeed been detached into the South Atlantic on a general
reconnaissance mission. The two much heavier Japanese
cruisers on station had moved out from Last Hope Inlet with
their landing craft some hours before *Briar* had got under
way and had then lain hove-to in blizzard conditions in the
western sector of the Magellan Strait, awaiting the return of
the *Sasebo* in relatively wide waters. As soon as the light
cruiser rejoined the squadron moved on ; *Sasebo*'s report had
been virtually useless. Her radar had packed up soon after
she had come out from the lee of Patagonia and the visibility
throughout had been such that her Captain had seen nothing,
though he had reported British W/T activity indicating a
strong presence likely to be in the Falklands. Rear-Admiral
Yamanaka, flying his flag in the cruiser *Ichikawa*, was not
unduly worried: he had enough strength himself and the
element of surprise was much in his favour. His most pressing
problem currently was pilotage in such terrible waters ....
When they began to approach the narrows he would send
away a boat to precede his ships through, taking soundings
continually and reporting back by means of flags. Yamanaka
paced his bridge anxiously ; it was not a pleasant job to take
heavy ships through the tricky channels behind Hoste Island
and the terrible Cape Horn, but he knew that much honour
would await him if he could come out so unexpectedly into
the South Atlantic to make all speed for the Falklands. His
Emperor would be pleased, and it was Admiral Yamanaka's

duty and pleasure to please Nihon-koku Tenno and to worship his ancestors who had sat on the Imperial throne of Japan before him. Emperor Hirohito was on this occasion acting in the interest of the German Führer, who wished as much interference as possible with the British convoys; Japan herself was unlikely to gain much benefit from the seizure of the wretched Falkland Islands, but the German Empire was Nihon-koku Tenno's ally and the orders had been given and that was that.

Yamanaka, half frozen on the open bridge, stared balefully at the dreadful desolation around him. Very primitive people lived here; Yamanaka had little time for either Chileans or Argentinians; neutrals in a world conflict were beneath the consideration of a warrior, and Admiral Yamanaka came from the Samurai tradition. All his ancestors had been warriors, as far back as they could be traced, which was virtually into the realms of mythology. He was a lover of war and all its glories, all its history, all its traditions of sacrifice and service, blood and steel and fire. He would have wished for nothing better than to die for his Emperor in war. And he had a personal loathing for the British as a race and for their Navy in particular.

There was a good reason for this.

In 1937 Rear-Admiral Yamanaka, then a commander, had been the Executive Officer of the heavy cruiser *Asigara* under Rear-Admiral Kobayashi and Captain Takeda at the review of the British Fleet held at Spithead in honour of the coronation of King George VI. The day before the review took place he had been invited with his Admiral and Captain to luncheon aboard the battleship *Nelson*, flagship of the British Home Fleet. Coming up the accommodation ladder to *Nelson*'s quarterdeck, climbing to the shrilling of the bosun's calls, he had naturally been at the tail of the line – rank went first out of a boat and he was the junior. The sound of the bosun's calls had died away and the words of welcome, haltingly uttered by a stupid British officer in atrocious Japanese,

121

had come to an end. As the visitors were escorted to the cabin of the British Commander-in-Chief, Home Fleet, Commander Yamanaka, whose English was impeccable, had caught a muted giggle and a muttered comment from a British Jack Tar . . . .

Yamanaka was a very short man, short even for a Japanese, one who found it difficult to peer above the bridge screen at sea, and he was sensitive about it. And the remark had been cruel in the extreme. The Jack Tar had said, very audibly, to a friend, 'Little yellow bugger's only two piss-pots high.'

Rear-Admiral Yamanaka's eyes shone and glittered with hate. He had never forgotten the moment, after all the years between. In a few days now he was going to have his revenge. The British and their piss-pots would be engulfed in a cataclysm.

11

ANOTHER crossing was made in the inflatable dinghies and the remaining explosives were brought safely ashore. Beaner was thoroughly chokker and said so to Leading Seaman Hoggett.

'Should have bloody joined the Army,' he said bitterly.

'Wish you had an' all. Then some dead unlucky corporal'd 'ave 'ad the bleedin' bother of you instead of me. Come on, get stuck in or I'll 'ave you.' Hoggett shivered; he didn't really blame Beaner for going bolshie. The wind was like a knife, a knife that cut right through into the bones. Much more of this lark and they would all end up with frostbite. The only thing was to keep busy, keep moving arms and legs and make the blood circulate. Hoggett looked across at Sub-Lieutenant Sykes; the officer seemed to be at his last gasp, just standing about and letting Gates take charge, which was probably just as well. Away to the right a sapper NCO was checking what was coming out of the dinghies, just like some kind of stores foreman – but no doubt the brown jobs had to account for everything down to the last toilet roll, just like in the Andrew. Lose a round of ammunition and you got hauled up, bollocked and charged with it off your pittance of pay. . . .

Hoggett saw Major Dixon striding over to Sykes, taking him by the arm and leading him aside, away from the others. Hoggett couldn't hear what took place but saw that Sykes wasn't liking it. Anyway, he seemed to take a grip after that and began shouting the odds in a hectoring voice.

123

'Come on, make it faster. The Major wants to get on the move. Leading Seaman Hoggett?'

'Yessir?'

'Take charge, can't you?'

Hoggett's mouth opened and shut again. Of all the insensitive cheek ... but you couldn't argue the toss with gold braid, they had you all the time, all ways up. Impertinence was a handy charge to get anybody on and it could lead swiftly to disrating. But a knot of anger hardened in Hoggett as he turned away and saw Beaner loafing again. 'Bloody little OD,' he said. 'It was *you* brought that load of crap down on me 'ead.'

Beaner grinned. 'Sorry, killick. I –'

'Just get on with it or you'll be sorrier.'

Beaner turned to. The dinghies were unloaded, deflated, folded and lifted between the seamen along with the explosives and rolls of fuse-line. Once again they slogged it out through the snow, over the rough ground, avoiding rocks, keeping their eyes watchful as more water came in due course into view. Dixon came down the struggling line with words of cheer.

'Not far now. The last stretch. Just keep it up a little longer. You've done splendidly, all of you. We're going to win if we make it in time.'

'Get stuffed,' Beaner said, *sotto voce*. He didn't really mean it; it was just an expression of his browned-off feelings. Being used as horses was what they were, mere beasts of burden for the soldiers. But he pushed on; maybe they would be given a stand-easy once they got there and he could have a fag – some hope! Not with all those explosives lying around. Beaner's mind flitted bird-like to his mate Quinn. He wondered how he'd made out after the snow started ... Quinn the keen, all-for-it volunteer. Probably regretted it by now. Everything in life was fate. If Quinn had waited for the call-up like Beaner, it could have changed the whole course of his service. Joining a year later, he might never have got a

124

draft chit to the *Briar* and wouldn't now be slogging his way through all that muck. It didn't do, to be keen.

Dixon had been right, however ; it wasn't far. Ten minutes later the halt was called and the weary men were fallen out, then immediately turned to again by Gates to carry the charges and fuses to where Dixon was all ready to lay them. Beaner stared up at the face of a mountain that was to be brought down to block the back end of the channel. For the first time, now he was there, he wondered what was to happen to the blowers-up once the Jap ships were in the net. They wouldn't just stand around aboard their useless, hemmed-in ships. They would pour ashore and seek out the men who'd done it to them.

Beaner, finding himself alongside Gates, made enquiries on the point.

Gates said briefly, 'No worries, Beaner. We bugger off fast.'

'Back to the ship ?'

'That's right.'

Beaner blew out his cheeks. Like the question of a fag : some hope ! There was a hell of a long way to go and they were already dead tired. The Japs would be fresh, and very, very angry.

Midshipman Carruthers was in a muck-sweat of indecision as he lay in his bunk. He'd spent much of the time either asleep or in a semi-comatose condition as a result of pain-killing drugs administered by Holtby, the SBA. In that somnolent state he'd thought back a lot to home and the easy pre-war life. He'd give anything to be back – mostly. But almost unknown to himself the war had changed him ; he had a suspicion it would never be quite the same again. After the war it wasn't going to be so easy ; the party spirit would have evaporated under the flame of a hard reality, of danger and death. The civilians were getting it too ; Reichsmarschal Goering was seeing to that, though he would be unlikely to

125

bother much with Northwood and Pinner. After the war . . .
so many girls were doing war work now, they wouldn't want
to go back to the social whirl as a full-time thing. No more
coffee parties in the morning, tennis in the afternoon, dances
in the evening – not every day like it used to be, anyway.

Life would change a lot.

He had no qualifications but would have to find a job.
Letters from home before they'd left Freetown had indicated
that his father's income had dwindled, partly because of
rising prices in the shops but also because there wasn't so
much coming in. His father had lost a lot of money . . . by the
time the war was over he would probably have lost a lot more
and wouldn't be able to support a work-shy son. That was one
thing; but there was another. The girls. Plenty of men would
be coming back from the war and heroes would be all the rage.
Men with good war records. If he tried to invent something,
he wouldn't be convincing – he knew that perfectly well.

And the questions . . .

What was your war like, they would ask.

Lying in my bunk when we met the Jap fleet. Bust my leg.
In action? Oh, no, I'd been swinging the lead because I was
scared, and fell arse over bollocks trying to make out I'd been
a conquering hero. Just ask Stripey Fish or Petty Officer
Lamprey – they know.

Carruthers' heart was like lead, the more so because he
very strongly suspected something. When the ship had been
in action against that Jap corvette, a sudden alteration of her
course had resulted in Carruthers' injured leg being rolled
heavily off the bunk, and he had fallen to the deck.

No extra pain, no sudden blinding agony. He'd lain there
wondering; the SBA had come in, clicked his tongue, and
lifted him back into his bunk. Carruthers hadn't said anything at the time but he was convinced his leg had not after all
been broken.

He ought to say so. He really ought . . . but that would
mean going back to duty most likely – say if the leg was only

sprained, or had a torn ligament. Say nothing and he was safe – so long as they didn't get sunk, of course, or a shell came through the bulkhead.

In actual fact, there was no safety anywhere aboard a ship. Carruthers thought about it, weighing the odds.

After the war was over . . . one day it would be. Then would come the reality, and that need to impress.

Carruthers brooded on ; finally he made up his mind. Next time the SBA came in Carruthers asked him a question. 'Holtby . . . how much do you really know about medicine ? I don't mean to be rude, but –'

'That's all right, sir,' Holtby said cheerfully. 'I don't know a lot. Enough to get by.'

'You weren't in it before the war ? A male –'

'Heavens, no. It's just the way the Service mind works, that's all. No, I was a bookie's runner . . . no scope for a bookie's runner in the Navy, see, so they made me an SBA.'

'Yes, I see,' Carruthers said carefully. 'In that case, you won't mind if I query your diagnosis?'

Fifteen minutes later, Midshipman Carruthers, his leg still heavily strapped and bandaged but no longer splinted, made a hazardous climb of the bridge ladder. He reported to the Captain. When his sudden recovery had been noted by the lower deck, Stripey Fish remarked that he had guts after all. He could have kept silent until this lot was over. Full marks to the Middy, Fish said. He had no sooner said this than there was a distant but very heavy explosion. It reverberated through the air for some two minutes and then there was silence.

Staff Sergeant Strong, in charge at the first explosion site to the east, had spotted the small ship's boat moving into the narrows. A lead was being cast and signals made by flag to something astern.

'Stand by, lads, this is it,' Strong said, crouched by his box of tricks out of sight from the water. He waited, heart pump-

127

ing fast. Into view came a Japanese cruiser, wearing what he took to be an admiral's flag. He placed a hand carefully on the firing plunger and went on waiting the right moment. Moving slowly and with extreme caution, the cruiser moved on below. Behind it came the assault force of landing ships, then another cruiser. Then a third. Strong could hear the subdued beat of the engines, echoing off the mountainside. There was the scent of victory . . . Strong's nostrils flared. *Give the buggers what for* . . . as the flagship came spot on, he took a deep breath, put both hands on the plunger, and rammed it down.

The world seemed to split open. An acrid stench swept back as flame erupted and the mountainside split asunder, hurling massive chunks of rock and many hundreds of tons of smaller debris smack on to the cruiser and down into the water all around her. Panic broke out. The ships astern reversed their engines just in the nick of time to avoid a pile-up. Strong peered cautiously from cover: on the flagship's bridge he could see a diminutive figure dancing with rage and shaking debris from his person. Half the bridge seemed to have gone; it had been laid wide open on the nearer side. One funnel had been sent sideways and smoke was issuing from a dozen cracks. A number of boats had been stove in and one of the twin 6-inch guns in the fore turret was pointing down into the fo'c'sle. And the ship was down by the head as though her bows had driven in hard, crunched into a bedrock of shattered mountain.

Bloody good-oh, Strong thought. But there was something wrong all the same. He turned to one of his sappers.

'Hear anything, did you?' he asked.

'*Hear* anything, Staff?' The sapper looked at him as if he'd gone round the bend.

Strong said impatiently, 'Not *this*! The western lot. Because I didn't. It's not gone up.'

Morgan said, 'That's the first, sir.' He waited, with Cameron.

Like Strong, they heard no more. Morgan said, 'They could have been simultaneous, I suppose.'

Cameron shook his head. 'I doubt it. Dixon was going to wait till he heard the first one, remember. The only way, in fact. I reckon we'd have heard two distinct explosions.'

'What the hell's happened, then?'

'No idea. I suggest one of two things: either the fuses or the charges themselves failed, or Dixon's lot were spotted.'

'Or they just didn't make it in time, sir.'

'Yes, all right – three possibilities. Perhaps yours is the most probable. Dixon's not likely to have ballsed up the job.'

'So what do we do?'

Cameron said, 'Head towards the second charge site, Pilot. We can assume the Japs have been caught by the first blow-up so we avoid that.'

'They'll come out astern, sir –'

'You mean we're likely to meet them. That's bloody true, but we've got to give the troops and our lads all the support we can,' Cameron said tersely. 'The situation's changed now. We can still hope to avoid the Japs . . . but whatever happens we have to try to operate a pick-up. Get a course laid off, Pilot.'

'Aye, aye, sir.' Morgan moved to the chart table and got busy with dividers and a parallel ruler. As he did so, the First Lieutenant came up the ladder and Cameron told him of the possibilities and what he intended to do.

'We may have to land, Number One. Get another party detailed and issued with rifles and bayonets. This time, you'll have to go ashore in charge – Carruthers is still hobbling about like a permanent cripple and I can't risk his leg packing up at the wrong moment.'

Frome nodded. 'Will you tell the ship's company the score, sir?'

'You can. Word of mouth. I'm not risking the tannoy – echoes could have a funny effect and I'm still hoping for at

129

least a degree of secrecy for a while. Pass the word round when you tell off the landing-party.' Cameron paused. 'And tell them this as well : we fight to the end. Last man and all that. I don't want to be melodramatic, but we've no option if we're spotted. Are you with me ?'

'All the way through,' Frome said, and turned away down the ladder. Cameron watched him go, wondering for how much longer they would remain an intact ship's company. He felt an immense depression : his word – *his* word for the first time – could send every man to his death if they met the Japanese guns. The little *Briar* wouldn't have a hope ; she would be blown clean out of the water at the first salvo, if the Japs even bothered to come broadside so as to fire all their guns. He had talked of turning and running ; it was the sane thing to do in the circumstances. But that wasn't how British Naval supremacy had been built up ; it wasn't how the out-gunned heroes of the war at sea to date had met the enemy : Kennedy, Warburton-Lee, Vian, Lord Louis Mountbatten to name a few. They'd gone right in and to hell with it. That was how wars were won and the *Briar* wasn't going to let anyone in the Fleet say she'd turned away. Not when it came to the point.

This sentiment was echoed in the wheelhouse by the coxswain, when the orders and the Captain's intentions came down to him through the voice-pipe. He asked one of his wheelhouse staff, 'Got a fag, Lofty ?'

'Sure, Chief.' A packet of Players was handed over.

Rodman blew a cloud of smoke. 'Could be the last, eh ? Or last but one.' He took two, putting the spare behind his ear, and handed the packet back. 'Tell you one thing, though: I'm glad the old *Briar* isn't going to show her arse to the enemy. Might give 'em ideas. I've heard yarns . . . the Japs almost make a religion of it.'

'Not the Japs, Chief. The Sikhs or someone . . . I reckon they regard it as obligatory – '

'Don't argue with your betters,' Rodman said with mock pomposity. 'It's only hearsay, whichever it is . . . .'

Dixon was in a controlled fury: if he'd been an RAF type he'd have blamed gremlins, but sappers had their feet on the ground. It was a burn fuse-line or something wrong with the firing box. Dixon got to work on it, seething with impatience, knowing he had to take it carefully. He believed, in fact, he would have time. The Japanese ships, the ones that could be presumed not to have grounded, wouldn't come charging backwards right away. They would do what could be done to succour their flagship first – unless they were ordered to leave her and go astern to carry out the mission on their own.

Dixon asked Sykes what his opinion was. This was more a matter of form; Sykes wouldn't have anything useful to say. He hadn't; he passed the query to Petty Officer Gates.

Gates said, 'Hard to say, sir. They may make an attempt to tow her off, that's assuming she *has* grounded which we don't know for sure.'

'If they do, what are the chances of success?'

'Depends on the damage and how hard aground she is,' Gates answered. 'It'd be a long job in any case, sir. If I was the Jap Admiral, well – I reckon I'd order the others out fast and try to get out on my own like. Lighten the ship – jettison as much as possible – go full astern with all hands mustered aft to lift her for'ard. And have 'em jumping up and down to shake the ship free.'

'Is that really done?' Sykes asked.

'Yes, sir,' Gates said. 'Hands to dance and skylark, that's the pipe.'

Dixon said, 'If you're right . . .' He looked at his watch. It was forty minutes now since the first explosion had been heard. The ships might perhaps come out faster than he'd thought if they met sea-room enough to turn and put their engines ahead. 'It begins to look like a cock-up.'

Gates asked, 'How's it going, sir? The fault?'

'It isn't, bugger it –'

'Could it be a break somewhere in the fuse-line itself? A break underneath the insulation –'

'If it is, my chaps haven't been able to isolate it,' Dixon said. 'There are alternative methods, but they're –' He broke off as a high shout came from Sykes. 'What the devil –'

'The Japs!' Sykes said. He pointed towards the east. A cruiser was moving into view and coming down fast towards the western narrows, taking full advantage of the sectors where speed was possible, and she was moving ahead. The turn had been made already. Gates reacted fast, shouting the Naval party into cover. Dixon cupped his hands and yelled out to his NCO. Some of the sappers, heads as it were buried in the job, were slow to respond. Dixon shouted again, telling them to hurry it up and vanish. Two men came down a slope at the rush, one of them carrying a spent reel of fuse-line. The hoods of their duffel-coats flew in the wind; beneath the hoods their British Army forage caps were visible to sharp eyes, eyes applied to binoculars. Abroad the cruiser a signal rating made a report to the Officer of the Watch. Within fifteen seconds small flashes were seen along the Japanese decks as the close-range weapons opened on the shore and the mountainside above the western narrows. Bullets swept across, sang like bees, sent slivers of rock zipping through the air to maim and kill. The ship came abeam, firing still, and passed through the narrows. Behind her a second cruiser was seen; and then the landing-craft. Gates lifted his head, watching for the landing-craft to come alongside and send their troops ashore. But the flotilla moved on, negotiated the narrows in safety towards open water. The firing was kept up. Lead seemed to be everywhere and Gates brought his head down again, fast, as a rock fragment flew past his ear. As the ships disappeared round a rocky promontory there was a silence, eerie and foreboding. Gates got to his feet. A little distance off, so did Sykes. And then Beaner and one or two others. A khaki forage cap

132

appeared cautiously from behind a rock, but there was no sign of Dixon or his NCO.

Unsteadily Sykes said, 'They've gone through.'

'Haven't they just,' Gates said, sounding bitter. 'It's a proper bollocks. Had 'em right in our grasp, we did.'

Sykes said, 'The map ... Major Dixon's. He showed me. There's more narrows ahead of them, to the west. But we'd never make it in time, of course.'

Gates was about to utter when the Japanese ships opened up again from around the far side of the jut of land. Heavier stuff, could even be the 6-inch turrets. Gates felt icy inside. Someone aboard those ships had guessed the score and in fact that didn't take too much doing in the circumstances. He opened his mouth and yelled, 'Get out of it, fast as you can,' and as he obeyed his own orders and ran blindly, stumbling and falling and getting to his feet again, the guns found their mark, found the laid charges, and the mountain opened in thunder and fury and a hail of riven rock.

12

THEY heard the racket aboard the corvette.

'A little late,' Frome said. 'But better late than never. Let's hope that's hemmed them in.'

Cameron said, 'Amen to that, Number One.' He moved across to the chart table, re-checked their course and the land contours that they would pass en route for the second firing position and the pick-up of personnel. Mostly the water was clear and wide ahead, just one narrow sector to pass through, beyond a jut of land, which could be the place Dixon had chosen for the second eruption of rock – or it could be the next along. It didn't matter which. Cameron felt rising excitement; it looked as though they'd brought it off, or anyway the troops had, his part had been small enough. To think of all those warships, hemmed in for the duration, ignominiously land-locked and helpless, left to rust away while their companies foot-slogged it across leagues and leagues of terrible country to surrender to a neutral power and be interned. The threat removed from the Falklands – at any rate until the Japs or maybe the Nazis tried again, but at least that day's action had given time for full preparation to repel an assault. And time was what the Falklands stood in need of; five thousand miles from Simonstown, three and a half thousand from Ascension, eight thousand from home waters. It was a long haul for reinforcements and supplies.

Stripey Fish, hearing the big blow-up, was exultant and expansive. 'Trust the boys in Navy blue, eh. *All the nice girls love a sailor, all the nice girls love a tar* . . . cor! When I gets back to Pompey –'

'More like bloody Freetown,' Leading Seaman Blanchard said, rolling a cigarette.

Fish disregarded him. 'When I gets back to Pompey the popsies'll go mad. This is going to make the newspapers . . . Jap Fleet Immobilized –'

'By Able Seaman Fish, I s'pose?'

'Not just me. Look, why deniggerate it? There's something to celebrate so why not –'

'Why not shoot a line, eh,' Blanchard said. He got to his feet. Three drags at his fag and he stubbed it out, shoving the remainder inside his cap for future use. He had to get back to his prisoners and tell them what had happened to their rotten fleet. He wouldn't be averse to a quiet gloat. As he went he whistled a tune, very flat, between his teeth. *And if it is a boy, send the bastard off to sea* . . . *the boys in Navy blue* . . . *climbing up the rigging like his daddy used to do* . . .

Behind his back, Fish stuck two fingers in the air. Leading hands were a pain in the neck. It hadn't been bloody Blanchard who'd shot down a Jap. If he, Fish, hadn't done that, the whole show might have gone very differently. Fish was prepared to bet a pound to a penny the skipper understood that if Blanchard didn't.

Once again, Gates lifted his head, having kept it down until some while after the world in his immediate vicinity had steadied. The whole local landscape seemed to have shifted. Half a mountain had gone, leaving a lot more sky. Gates stood up and felt himself all over. Nothing broken, but some blood from lacerations, nothing to get excited about. Here and there heads poked up and Gates became aware of cries.

He took a deep breath and looked all around. Harshly he called out, 'Anyone that can stand, get on his feet. There's work to do. Rescue work. Anyone seen Mr Sykes?'

There was no answer. One by one the men mustered, look-

135

ing at one another in awe. Beaner emerged, white and shaken and with what Gates considered a loony look in his eye. Shell-shock or something like. Tears were rolling down Beaner's face.

'Take a grip, Beaner,' Gates said, sounding fierce for Beaner's own good. 'You're alive. Some aren't and some are injured. Where's Hoggett?'

'Here, PO.'

Gates swung round on his heel. 'Right. Gather the hands together and look lively. Not much we can do except try to dig out those that's buried.' He asked again about Sykes. No one had seen the officer. There were three sappers left, no NCO, no Dixon. Gates gathered the army into his fold and they set to work. They found Dixon, cut slap through the middle, probably sawn into by a flying jag of rock. Gates felt sick. He'd seen similar aboard a ship more than once, but he had never got used to it. Four more bodies were found, Naval ones. Some of the injured were in a bad way, not long to go and nothing at hand to make it easy. As they were dug out by scrabbling hands and the points of the bayonets Gates was further sickened by the sounds they made. Piteous cries, moans, screams as they were hauled clear. Maybe it was the wrong thing, but what else could you do? Couldn't just leave them, had to do something – if only to ease your own conscience. There was a lot in that; like the way you'd probably try to stop a suicide, you didn't really think about the person concerned.

Gates tried to shut his ears to the cries. They made him feel murderous, shook his ability to do his job properly. *Why couldn't they bloody shut up?*

'You there! *Beaner!*'

Beaner swayed but didn't answer.

'Hurt, are you? Let's have a look.' Gates approached him, felt for broken bones though he knew there weren't any from the way Beaner was able to move. 'No damage fleshwise?'

Beaner just stared. Gates reckoned the hurt was in his

mind, nowhere else. That loony look ... Gates was no doctor and did the only thing he knew: gave Beaner the sharp edge of his tongue, doing his best to shake him out of it. Then he said, 'Right, Beaner. Fossick around and find Mr Sykes, right? *Move!*'

Keep him occupied, that was the thing. Take his mind off his own self. Beaner moved away as if in a dream, wandering about in the general shatter and stench of explosive that hung like a cloud. Gates turned to again with the rest of the fit hands, not many of them, and didn't stop until he'd accounted for as many as possible. Some just weren't there at all – buried too deep to be got at, Gates guessed, or they'd been blown to fragments too small to see. The light was going from the sky now and that didn't help. Soon it would be pitch dark. Pitch dark, and out on a limb not so far off bloody Antarctica. And as for the Japs ...

At Gates' feet something lay: an officer's cap badge on its black mohair band. Sykes.

Gates picked it up and looked around. No cap to be seen. Well, explosions did funny things, no accounting for them. *Very* funny things. Gates was about to walk away when he heard a weak voice.

'Petty Officer Gates ...'

'Yes! Where, for Christ's sake ...' Gates stopped and looked around. It was uncanny, as though Sykes was yacking from the other side of a curtain, or veil or whatever. 'Where the fuck *are* you, sir?'

'Here.'

Gates turned again, like a spinning top. Then he saw two large segments of rock that looked as though they'd been part of the mountain – the split had a sort of fresh look. In the cleft between them, covered with debris, something stirred. Sykes. Gates ran across and scrabbled at loose rubble and the officer emerged. 'You've been lucky,' Gates said. It looked as though the two pieces of mountain had dropped slap on either side, leaving Sykes undamaged. And undamaged he was; he sat up, shivering and wild-eyed, not unlike Beaner.

'You all right, sir?'

'Yes. Yes, I'm all right.'

'Glad to hear it. We're in a spot, sir.'

'I expect we'll be found . . . don't you think?'

Gates said, 'I don't reckon too much on that. The skipper, he won't know where we are, not for sure anyway. And there's another thing, isn't there?'

'What?'

'The Japs. If the skipper moves this way, he's likely to run slap into 'em. Or come to that, *any* way he goes.'

'If he leaves the inlet, yes.' Sykes rubbed at his eyes. 'He may not, you know. We just don't know, do we – but perhaps we ought to try to reach the ship.'

Gates shook his head. 'No, sir. Not make for the inlet, anyway. See it from the skipper's angle. He's had no report following the first explosion. I reckon he'll think something's up – which it is, now. We're marooned here and the Japs have gone. He won't know *that*, of course, but after two explosions and no word I reckon he's going to get under way. Bound to.'

'In case we need help?'

'Yes,' Gates said impatiently. 'Stands to reason. We're best off here, anyway through the night. That's my opinion.' He paused. 'But there's one other thing: those Japs. Two cruisers went through, with the landing-craft flotilla. Now, there may have been more ships. Major Dixon, he believed the leading ship would go aground. And when the cruisers passed us, I didn't see any admiral's flag, did you, sir?'

'No. No, I don't think I did.'

Think, think, Gates thought furiously, it's up to an officer to *know*. One thing the sea taught you was to use your eyes, but it hadn't taught Sykes anything. Gates said forbearingly, 'Well, then! Maybe the flagship's stuck on her arse on the

138

rock, back east. Look, sir. Do you happen to know the full strength of that assault squadron? If you do, now's the time to say so.'

'Yes . . .'

'Yes, what, for Christ's sake?'

Sykes said, 'I do know. Or rather, I know there was a signal from the Admiralty. They believed there were more ships than originally notified.'

'Right! Well, I reckon the flagship *is* still there, hemmed in beyond the first blow-up area – right in it, in fact. That being so –'

'We may come under attack?'

Gates nodded. 'Got it in one, sir. Brilliant! For my money, the Jap Admiral, he'll be doing his nut. As soon as he heard that second big bang, if not before, he'll have landed a party if only to find out what's going on. They'll come this way because the bang was this way, right? And we're likely to be heavily outnumbered. We have two courses of action, if I may suggest them.'

'Go on.'

Gates said heavily, 'One, we get as far west as we can and hope the Japs won't advance beyond the explosion point, that is, here. Two, we dig in defensively and take as many of the sods with us as possible. Well? Your decision, sir. Not mine.'

Rear-Admiral Yamanaka's mood was very much as forecast by Petty Officer Gates. To be hard aground was an undignified situation for any Flag Officer and Yamanaka was furious at British duplicity. That word of his mission against the Falkland Islands had leaked was obvious; he might very well be blamed personally for that. He had perhaps allowed his squadron to be observed by ill-disposed persons in the neutral South American countries, persons who had lost no time in informing the British. Of course, that had been a risk all along, one he had foreseen and had brought to the atten-

139

tion of his superiors but to no avail. They had scarcely listened to him but would still blame him now that things had gone wrong.

Rear-Admiral Yamanaka stared disconsolately down his flagship's side. Huge chunks of rock lay all around him, and underneath him too. He had tried everything: engines ahead with their powerful thrust, trying to heave his command over the wretched obstructions brought down by the British, so that he could move ahead towards his ultimate objective. That had been rash. The flagship had become more stuck. Yamanaka had seethed, seeing himself surrounded by sycophantic fools who hadn't dared to tell him he had been wrong to try it. Then astern: a great boiling-up of water and that had been all.

No movement. Even worse; the screws had eventually become damaged when they had bitten into rock, and his main shafts had almost been twisted into knots as the screws suddenly stopped with the engines at Full Astern. There had been panic sounds from his chief engineer officer. They had worsened Yamanaka's vicious mood and he had been tempted to put the engineer officer under arrest, but had resisted. There had been the question of a tow; but Yamanaka didn't believe that would have a hope of success since there was as much rock astern as ahead – he had realized now that he was right in the middle of the pile. And he preferred to send the rest of his squadron away in case further damage was brought about by the British, or perhaps they were Americans, before his ships could move to safety.

Loudly, Rear-Admiral Yamanaka ordered a landing-party to be mustered and put ashore to carry out an exhaustive search of the area and apprehend the enemy. He padded up and down his bridge, eyes bright with hate. Once caught, the foreign devils would face questioning and then death. He would tame their arrogance .... Yamanaka was thinking back to the British Fleet Review in 1937. The British were mostly tall men. Except the great Admiral Nelson ... Yam-

140

anaka's walk became more dominant and his shoulders went back. He took up a position a moment later where there was less bridge screen in the way to obscure his view of the shore.

Briar's speed had been reduced as the chart showed the start of shoaling water. Soundings were being taken by Leading Seaman Blanchard, relieved from POW guard duties in order to man what would in a bigger ship have been the chains. He was swinging his lead efficiently, a beautiful cast of which he was proud, arm held straight to send the lead-line well ahead of the corvette. He sang out the depth of water, back to the Captain and navigator on the bridge.

Cameron and Morgan, the lookouts and the leading signalman were watching closely, all around the ship. There was no sign of any enemy. They might have been in a world of their own, in a sea on a distant planet. The snow apart, the very landscape looked like the popular idea of somewhere akin to Mars. Great peaks, jagged rocks, lurid colours as the sun went down the sky -- it was sheer beauty, but cruelty lurked, the cruelty of bitter weather, and somewhere behind it all the barbarity of the guns.

'Still no aircraft,' Cameron said.

'Yes. Odd, isn't it, sir?'

Cameron nodded. No doubt there were reasons and he was only too thankful not to come under attack from the air. One explanation might well be that the Japanese carrier was already on its supportive way around Cape Horn – but no: it wouldn't be. It was believed to be waiting to give its support once the main assault force was approaching the Falklands. The whole point of the Japanese manoeuvre, the approach through the network behind Hoste Island, was to lessen the chances of being observed by any British warships. The carrier would still be somewhere in the far south of the Pacific, waiting her moment ... general considerations of security might well be the reason for her not flying off any more of her aircraft ....

Morgan said, 'Those Jap cruisers, sir. If they're slap between the two explosions, I wonder they haven't at least tried to get a wireless message through and never mind the land configuration. They'll know their movements are no longer secret.'

Cameron noded; the W/T was keeping a guard on transmissions but nothing had been picked up although they were covering all likely frequencies. He said, 'The Japs will know there's not been any other wireless activity in the area – the Admiral may see a value in preserving his secrecy in the wider sense.'

'Fat lot of good if he's hemmed right in. If he is, he'll never get out again short of bringing in heavy clearance teams, dredgers, cranes, the lot.' Morgan paused. 'It makes me wonder if he *is* hemmed in, sir.'

'Something may have gone adrift, Pilot, but it makes no odds in regard to the Japs not transmitting. If they were under way as planned, they certainly wouldn't be putting anything out over the air.'

Morgan grunted. The Captain was right, but Morgan felt distinctly uneasy without being able to lay a precise finger on the cause. Maybe it was just the fact that there was too much apparent peace around, peace that he believed to be no more than skin deep. In some respects it was like a pre-war cruise of the northern fjords, gin-palacing around Norwegian waters. Plenty of people would pay good money for this, at any rate until the snow came back.

A little later the entry to the first of the narrows loomed ahead of the corvette. Cameron reduced speed still further, and called the engine-room.

'Chief, bridge here. We're about to enter the narrows.'

'Aye, aye, sir.'

Cameron straightened. Another half mile and he would have to turn to starboard into the enclosing land mass, making his entry between great mountain faces. The pilotage would be tricky to say the least; and now it was almost dark which would increase the difficulties. Not as yet too dark to see the entrance. . . .

Cameron brought up his glasses and examined the approaching channel. Something was stirring . . . he gave an exclamation and said to Morgan, 'D'you see what I see, Pilot ?'

Morgan looked to where Cameron was pointing. He said in a low voice, 'By God I do ! Masts and fighting-tops . . .'

They were on the move: something, undoubtedly, had gone wrong.

13

SYKES had been in a muck-sweat of indecision, even the cold forgotten in the over-riding urgency of making a choice between what he saw as two evils. To head west might be of no help at all ; they might become hopelessly lost or the Japs would pursue them to the bitter end and then it would be all up with them all. But to stay and fight would equally be the end. There were not enough of them and there would be literally hundreds of Japanese available to the flagship.

He said, 'We've no maps now.'

Gates nodded. The maps had gone with Dixon. He'd made a search and found nothing ; they had no doubt been buried deep under the piles of rubble. All the same, Gates' instinct was to head west. He, as much as Sykes, knew the odds against them if they made a stand.

'My advice is, sir,' he said, 'to put as much distance between us and them as possible.'

'Yes . . .'

'We may get away with it, we may not. But it gives us a chance.' Gates looked down at the officer and clicked his tongue. 'Speed's the thing now. Care to give the order, would you, before it's too bloody late ?'

Sykes wasted no more time. Gates was an experienced man. He said, 'Yes, all right. We'll head west.'

Gates let out a long breath, turned about and shouted, 'Right, you lot. On your feet ! We're moving out.' He de-

tailed four men. 'You and you and you and you. Inflatable
dinghies – sort out the ones that aren't bloody punctured and
bring 'em – you never know, we might even find the ship by a
miracle.'

Ordinary Seaman Beaner was one of the hands detailed.
He was still in a daze and was all thumbs. Somehow, in spite
of Beaner, they sorted out the dinghies. Just two were still
usable. This done, they moved out. It was desperately hard
going ; no explosives to carry now, but there were the injured
men as well as the dinghies. Under Gates' instructions, the
hands took turns with the burden. Gates was everywhere at
once, exhorting, rasping, lending a hand himself. Sykes
stumbled along, a picture of misery and woe. They were all
done for. Gates had been talking nonsense, of course, about
finding the ship. Without maps or charts, they hadn't a hope.
They were all going to die in this dreadful frozen wilderness.
Like Carruthers earlier, Sykes was visited by home thoughts.
The semi in Twickenham – paradise wasn't the word. God ! If
only he'd been in a reserved occupation he'd be there still,
going down to the pub and all that. Some people were born
lucky. It wasn't fair. Sykes knew any number of people who
hadn't been called up and they were making a good thing of
it, making more money than they'd ever made in their lives
till the war came. There were any number of fiddles on the
black market, plenty of good rackets going. He'd even have
paid off the mortgage most likely, and who was going to pay
it off after he'd died down here at the world's end ? The wife
would have a hard time of it and she wouldn't get any help
just because he'd died on active service. Fight for your
country – yes, but they don't give you any of it afterwards.
Patriotism was bunk. Sykes stumbled on and on and on and
once again the wind caught them as they came to higher
ground, out of the lee of the peaks in the quarter where the
wind was. The fallen snow swirled, was blown cruelly into
Sykes' face. He adjusted his scarf and hood but it didn't seem
to make much difference.

Gates battled up alongside him, determinedly cheerful. 'All right, are you, sir?'

Sykes didn't answer; he couldn't bring himself to. He felt close to tears of desperation and self-pity. He detested Gates. He knew what Gates thought of him. Gates went on. He said, 'Not far to go now.' The dark was coming down, but Gates had caught the gleam of water ahead, had seen that they were approaching an arm of the land and that it was surrounded by that water, down below them. 'Not far to go, and no bugger chasing us. Not yet, that is. Want to bet, sir?'

Sykes licked his lips, forced himself for dignity's sake to make some response. 'What on?'

'That we'll pull through, that's what on.' Gates' voice was crisp. 'We'll make it, don't you fret.'

'I'm not fretting.'

'No. No, of course you're not, Mr Sykes.'

'But you think I am, don't you?'

Gates' breath hissed out. 'Not on your life. Not more'n the rest of us. None of us likes it, sir. We just put up with it. Maybe I said the wrong thing. I –' He broke off, put a hand on Sykes' arm. 'Down, sir! *Get down!*'

'What –'

'Jap cruisers, sir, the two that escaped the trap like – coming up right below us. Don't want to be seen, do we?' As Sykes went flat in the snow, Gates called to the rest of the party, sending them on to their stomachs. Funny, he thought, that the land sloggers had overtaken the Jap ships ... but maybe not so odd at that. The Japs, they'd have been going slower than dead slow, obviously, in these rotten tricky waters, and besides, it was likely the party had come by a more direct route – the channel, for all Gates knew, could twist about all over the place.

Sykes asked, 'I suppose that's the narrows ahead?'

Gates nodded. 'I reckon so. The last of 'em. And the sods are moving through – and bugger-all we can do about it.

146

Except maybe take a few pot shots at the bridge personnel. They'd be just about within rifle range, I reckon.'

'No point, is there?'

Gates gave him a sidelong look. 'Not much, no. Just a case of satisfaction. It wouldn't exactly stop 'em, I agree. Wouldn't help 'em either, though, if we knocked off the navigating officers, say, just when they're coming up to the trickiest part.'

'Suicide on our part.'

Gates said, 'We *are* fighting a war, sir. I'd say it was our duty if you asked me, which you haven't.'

'No, I haven't.'

'Go out in glory, sir?'

Sykes trembled. He said, 'We don't have to "go out" at all. You said we'd come through. There's no point in heroics. A handful of men against two cruisers! It's – it's insane!'

Gates said, 'I s'pose you call yourself a man.'

'You've no right –'

'Look, sir. Somewhere beneath all that wool, there's a gold stripe. That's an honourable thing to wear, or always has been. If you want to go through life knowing that a bunch of the lads know you're bloody yellow, well, that's your affair, not mine. I wouldn't like to live with it, I can tell you that. Want your kids to be proud of you, don't you? You've got the chance now. You won't have it much longer.' Gates pointed. 'Those cruisers are moving further out. If you don't give the order within five seconds, I will. Got it, have you?'

'You bastard.'

Gates grinned. 'Hard words break no bones, that's what they say.' He half rose to his feet and crawled away. Sykes heard him passing the orders, saw the Naval party crawl towards the lip of what looked like a gorge, bringing the Japanese cruisers and landing ships below the sights of their rifles. Gates was in the lead and had discarded his revolver

147

in favour of a rifle. Gates happened to have the crossed rifles of a good shooting badge on his cuff, and knew he'd be a better prospect than most of the lads. Sykes saw him bring his rifle up and squint along the sights.

On the corvette's bridge, Cameron had his own moment of indecision as the cruisers were seen ahead. Through his mind ran Nelson's signal at Trafalgar: *Engage the enemy more closely*. But Nelson's fleet had been the equal of the combined French and Spanish sail-of-the-line. One corvette against powerful, heavily gunned cruisers was a flea against leviathans and never mind what he'd said on his bridge earlier. Had he the moral right to throw away his ship's company when it came to the crunch? For throwing away it would be. He could achieve absolutely nothing by staying and fighting and it was perfectly possible the ship hadn't yet been seen from the Japanese squadron. They could still turn away and hide up until the heavy ships had gone.

But there was something craven in that.

Meanwhile Morgan was waiting for orders, his eyebrows raised interrogatively at the Captain, his body bent ready to pass the orders down to the coxswain.

Cameron was looking towards the narrows through his binoculars. Still he gave no order. As all the alternatives swarmed in his consciousness there was a dot-and-carry-one step on the ladder: Carruthers.

'Captain, sir –'

'Yes, what is it?'

'I've had an idea, sir. I saw the Japs . . . and it seemed to me we might be able to use the depth charges, sir.'

Cameron stared. 'Depth charges, for God's sake! We're not up against a submarine, Mid!'

'No, sir. I didn't mean that – not to try to sink them. Depth charge the exit, sir. Hope to block them in. There might just be time if we hurry, sir.'

Cameron rubbed at his eyes, which were stinging with

tiredness. Depth charges. There was – there might be – something in it. The throwers, projecting the TNT up and sideways as part of the pattern, might well bring down quite a solid amount of rock. He gave a sudden grin. 'Mid, you're a bloody marvel! It's worth a try.'

'Yes, sir. There's another thing. We're short of torpedomen for the depth charges, sir – most of them went with the landing-parties . . . I'll have a go, sir, if that's all right. I – I'd like to do something to –'

'If you think you can do it, Mid, have a go. I'll be relying on you.' Cameron leaned from the bridge rail, looking aft. 'Number One!'

Frome lifted a hand. 'Sir?'

'Stand by depth charges. Carruthers is on his way down. Muster all hands that are left of the depth-charge party.' Cameron went back to the fore part of the bridge. 'Pilot, bring her round, full helm. We make a stern approach – we don't want to seal ourselves in as well.'

'Wheel hard-a-starboard,' Morgan said down the voicepipe. He watched the ship's head closely. 'Midships . . . steady.'

'Engine to Full Astern,' Cameron said.

Bells rang; a kerfuffle of water built up aft, and foam started to move for'ard as the corvette gathered her sternway, backing up fast to the entrance. They were little more than a quarter of a mile off now and two cruisers were coming into full view, bearing down at dead slow speed in the narrowest part. It was dark now; the Japanese were mere shapes, huge moving masses in the night. It was just possible the men on their bridges had seen nothing of the blacked-out corvette yet – just possible.

But *Briar*'s luck was out.

As they all watched, as the tension grew unbearably, as the little corvette went on astern for her firing position, a flash was seen from the leading ship's fore turret: twin 6-inch guns had opened fire. The projectiles came close above the bridge,

149

took the water well past the corvette's bows. The Japanese hadn't got the range but it could be only a matter of minutes now. Cameron's heart pumped ; he found himself praying for a little more time, time enough for him to release his depth charges in the proper place. It was all a question of time now : time before they went up in a roar of flame from the heavy batteries, time before the leading cruiser reached the exit and passed through in safety. The wait was agonizing. *More speed* ... but down below in what could so soon become a blazing hell, Chief ERA Parbutt was doing his level best to give him every possible knot that could be squeezed from his puny engine.

They waited for the next lot of projectiles to scream towards them. But before they came there was a diversion. The leading signalman was the first to hear it and report.

'Rifle-fire, sounds like, sir. From the land, high up.'

'*Rifles* ... can you see anything, Black ?'

'Not a sausage, sir. Just heard it, that's all. I reckon it's the landing-party, sir. Must be. There it goes again.'

This time, Cameron heard it. Then the next heavy shells were sent screaming towards them. More flashes ; and the projectiles came close on either beam. Huge spouts of water lifted, sent solid sea over the corvette, drenching the bridge, drenching the gun's crew for'ard and the depth-charge party aft. Everything in the ship semed to ring and a shudder went through her plates. In the engine-room Parbutt was flung from the starting-platform and fetched up on his backside on the steel deck, cursing vividly. He got up and went back, clutching his rump. On the bridge the report came in from Midshipman Carruthers.

'Depth charges ready, sir.'

Cameron acknowledged. 'Well done, Mid. Stand by. It won't be long now.'

'Aye, aye, sir.' Aft, Carruthers was in a state of high excitement. Some instinct was telling him it was going to be all right. And the something that had got into him when he'd found his leg wasn't broken after all, when he'd had that good look at himself and his past and future – that was still with him. He was going to make a good fist of the time he spent in the Navy. Now was his chance. It was going to be a pretty big thing, to put the final seal on a Japanese cruiser squadron and a bunch of assault craft.

He waited, trembling with his anticipation, for the final order. Alongside him Stripey Fish, co-opted into the depth-charge party for what might be *Briar*'s last act, and in Stripey's mind would be, considered death. He might be flung clear if he was lucky. The water would be bloody perishing, of course, but he'd heard it said that fat men could survive it longer than skinny ones, all bone. Stripey patted his gut ; for the first time in his life he gave thanks for it. All those jokes in the past – it was going to be him who had the last laugh now. Perhaps. He might get blown to smithereens and that was different. But everyone had to die sometime and Fish began all at once to feel philosophical about it. At least it would be quick, bloody fast. There was another funny thing : him and young Carruthers, just about the most useless articles in the ship – odd how you saw things clear when it was on the cards you were going to die – fit only for searchlight duty in action but now about to help God save England.

You never knew how things were going to turn out.

As, unknown to Stripey Fish, Sub-Lieutenant Sykes had also discovered a little earlier.

Just as Petty Officer Gates had got his aim, tragedy had come to him. The overhanging lip of what was virtually a precipice gave way ; Gates was unable to save himself and no one near him reacted in time. He went over, spread-eagled, his rifle falling away clear of his body. No-one heard his end ; it was a long drop and death came instantaneously.

A man got up and ran back to Sykes, who was lying on his stomach in rear.

'Petty Officer Gates, sir. Gone over, sir.'

'Bloody hell!' Sykes put his head in his hands, feeling his guts turn over. Now he was on his own, no one to turn to. Poor Gates ... whatever he'd been like ... he'd been a stiffener.

The man – it was Beaner – was waiting for orders. *His* orders, unsupported and not forced upon him by Gates. Beaner said, 'Call if off, sir? Lie doggo?' He sounded hopeful.

Sykes remembered all that Gates had said. Somehow the fact that Beaner was there in front of him, as shit-scared as he was and as wishful to lie doggo – Beaner, seeing him as the soft option, the officer who would cave in and let himself as well as the rest off the hook – it all did something for Sykes. He said, 'That's no good, Beaner. Gates ... the Japs will have seen what happened, very likely, so it's too late. Open fire immediately. Point of aim the bridge of the leading ship.'

14

'WHY don't the skipper get on with it?'
Stripey Fish asked rhetorically. Carruthers saw no need for
an answer, wasn't really capable of giving one. Talk about
close – they were in fact almost close enough now to the
leading cruiser for the latter's guns to be unable to depress
far enough. There was some safety in that. But now there
were faces looking down from the great, rearing bow where
one anchor was lowered to the waterline, ready for letting go
if required in narrow waters.

'Rifles,' Fish said, and dodged backwards fast. Bullets
snicked the depth charges. At the same time more firing was
heard from the heights to starboard of the channel entry.
Neither Carruthers nor Fish could see what was going on. On
the bridge Cameron had no better view. But he noted the
result of that invisible rifle fire when through his binoculars
he saw the glass screen of the cruiser's bridge shatter. This he
saw clearly in the back-glow of a searchlight that had come
on to probe the land to the port side of the cruiser. The
bridge seemed to be in chaos; and the moment had now
come to send off the depth charges.

Cameron passed the order aft.

Carruthers reacted instantly. *Fire depth charges!* A
moment later he spun round, a hand clutching his shoulder.
Blinding pain . . . this time the wound was real enough. But
he took a grip and carried on. Short-handed as they were, he
had to do the job of a seaman torpedoman. With Fish, he

fired off the charges, opening the stern racks, operating the throwers to port and starboard, the shallowest possible settings already on the pistols of the canisters. Then he reported to the bridge. He was ordered to get all hands for'ard as fast as possible. When he turned to pass the order to Stripey Fish, he found that Fish had gone already. Making his way for'ard himself, Carruthers slipped in a trail of blood and went headlong. A moment later the Japanese bullets got him. His body moved violently and then lay still. A little further along the deck, Fish lay just as dead. He had managed to crawl some distance from the rifles but hadn't quite made it.

On the bridge, Cameron ordered Full Ahead and started praying, hands over his ears and head down. Morgan was crouching behind the binnacle – the ship was all right pilotage-wise, there was a clear run ahead for long enough. Morgan was counting the seconds, wondering when the end would come. You didn't normally drop charges in shallow water, nor in closely land-locked water either. There was no knowing what the result might be.

Sykes had gone down as close as he dared to the lip of the cliff. He was feeling the excitement now, able to visualize the consternation on the cruiser's bridge as the nerve centre of ship-handling came under fire. The second cruiser and the assault craft were coming up below now, and the rifle fire was being returned by the close-range weapons but with no effect whatsoever. The seamen were keeping back from the edge and were protected, such was the enforced angle of fire, by the cliff itself. Leading Seaman Hoggett, who had sent Beaner to get Sykes' order, was not so far behind Gates in rifle proficiency. He fired fast but unhurriedly, helped rather than hindered by the searchlight beams, which seemed unable to pick up their target. Before the leading cruiser had passed out of effective range he and the other ratings had fired slap down into the compass platform. Hoggett was sure they'd made a clean sweep of the bridge personnel.

Bad for a ship in pilotage waters . . .

Hoggett grinned savagely as he rammed home another clip and worked the bolt of his rifle and carried on firing, taking the next ship now. With the officers of the leading ship gone, the quartermaster down in the wheelhouse would be blind and wouldn't be getting any orders. In which case he would do all he could do: hold his course. The result of that was likely to be chaos, since just before the narrow exit to open water, the channel took a bend. Not much, but enough. That would be a lovely sight to watch. Lovely for the skipper too. Hoggett believed that the heavy gunfire that had opened after the leading ship passed out of his target area might well indicate the presence of the corvette outside the narrows.

'All right, Beaner?'

'Sure.'

'I reckon,' Hoggett said, 'it's going our way. Just you watch. Grandstand view, anyway of the arse-end Charlies.' He paused. 'How was Sykes?'

Beaner grinned. 'All for it, I reckon.'

'Never!' Squinting through his sights, Hoggett reflected on Sykes. Funny the way things went. He'd been dead astonished when Beaner had brought the order to open fire instead of the order to scarper. But maybe Sykes never had been an actual coward; just dim and far from keen .... Hoggett forgot Sykes as happy things started happening below. He got to his feet for a better look and called to Beaner.

'Now just watch,' he said again.

Briar reacted to the explosions of the depth charges as though she had been struck by a tidal wave. Her stern came up and her bow went down, and she rolled and shuddered, ringing in every plate, seeming to spring every rivet in her construction. The engine-room felt to Parbutt as though it had turned turtle. There was a hollow din like a bell tolling, and everything seemed to dance away from the bulkheads, but there was no apparent damage. On the bridge Cameron was flung back against the binnacle and landed in a heap, together with Morgan and Leading Signalman Black. The starboard lookout went clean over the guardrail and smacked down in a boiling sea. Astern all hell had been let loose. In a fraction of time before the charges went up Cameron had noticed the bows of the leading cruiser paying off a little to port and heading dangerously inshore towards the jags of rocks sticking up from the water. When he pulled himself to his feet and looked back the contours of the channel entry had altered to quite some extent and a good deal of mountain had plummeted down to the cruiser's upper deck, smashing the close-range weapons and wireless and radar aerials. In the glow of one remaining searchlight she looked like an abandoned quarry.

Cameron said, 'Slow ahead, Pilot. Bring her round.'

The corvette's way eased and she came round to starboard. Cameron ordered the engine stopped. Some eight cables'-lengths short of the entry he brought the ship up with a touch astern on the engine, and she lay peacefully as the kerfuffle subsided. Cameron and Morgan stared in awe.

'What a bloody shambles,' Morgan said. 'Just bloody look what we've gone and done !'

'Not just us. The charges might not have been enough for all we know.'

'The landing-party, sir ?'

Cameron nodded. 'That cruiser slewed right off course because she was no longer under full command.' He looked closely through his binoculars : the leading ship was laid smack across the channel, acting as her own blockship, jammed between the rocks, bows and stern well dug in, smashed beyond any chance of local repair. Steam was pouring from what looked like a hundred apertures, and as Cameron watched the drama brought itself to its own conclusion. The next ship in the line, her bridge personnel lying dead at their stations, had failed to react in time. Her knifing bows crunched into the side of the leader, driving in hard and forcing the inert cruiser deeper into the rocks. Shouts and cries came back to the corvette, and more steam spurted. The ships' own searchlights gave vivid light to the scene.

Morgan said, 'If you're right it looks like one up to Dixon, sir.'

'Yes. Or Sykes.'

Morgan looked sideways, quizzically. 'Or Sykes indeed,' he said. He checked an unfavourable reference to Sykes. There was no need to be uncharitable until they knew all the facts, and Sykes could have pulled his socks up under pressure. He said, 'Now we have to get them back, sir. It's not going to be easy. What do we do about the Japs?'

'Outflank them if we can, Pilot. Find an inlet in rear of where the firing came from. We may not get all that much interference – those Japs are pretty well tied up one way and another!'

Morgan grinned and moved across to the chart table. Cameron followed. 'There,' Morgan said. He indicated a narrow waterway running parallel with the channel where the crippled ships were locked in. 'Just enough water to take us. Put a party ashore sir?'

'Yes. The party already detailed to land. First Lieutenant in charge.' Cameron looked up as rifle fire came from the ship across the entry. 'They're waking up. Let's get out.'

'Let's get out,' Sykes also said at about the same moment. 'No more we can do now.'

'True enough, sir.' Hoggett turned to the landing-party and the handful of sappers: while the shooting had been going on two men from the first explosion site had come in, dragging themselves with difficulty over the hard, snow-covered ground. They had reported the rest killed when the Japanese had mounted a land attack from the flagship. There had been a tough fight and Staff Sergeant Strong had bought it, just a few seconds after he had ordered the two survivors to beat it and report to the Navy. Now, Leading Seaman

157

Hoggett knew there was nothing left to wait for. 'Right, you lot,' he said. 'We're moving out.'

'How?' Beaner asked pointedly.

Hoggett looked at Sykes. Sykes said, 'I don't know.'

'There's one thing for sure,' Hoggett said, 'and that is, it's not over yet. Down there, there's a lot of annoyed Japanese persons, sir. The ships may be stuck, but *they* bloody aren't. Nor are their guns, not necessarily. So what do we do, eh?'

'Well ... we could go back to where the second lot of charges were laid. That's where *Briar* may head.'

'No, sir. The skipper's *here* – or so I reckon. All that gunfire. That's if 'e hasn't bin blown up. If I might make a suggestion, sir, I reckon we'd best try to find a way down right where we are now. *That* way.' Hoggett pointed towards the south away from the Japanese warships, sighing inwardly. Sykes was still a right prat, thought of nothing in advance, didn't use his loaf, couldn't make up what he probably thought of as his mind. 'An' lose no time about it, sir.'

'Yes,' Sykes said uncertainly. He looked around. It was very dark, but there was a glow from the searchlights that lit the scene below the peaks and it gave him enough light to appreciate what seemed to be the hopelessness of their situation. One way was as good, or as bad, as another. The first thing to do was to see if they could find a track of some sort. Hoggett didn't think it likely; the place was uninhabited and probably had been so from the dawn of history.

'Ever done any mountaineering, sir?' he asked. Sykes hadn't; neither had anyone else in the Naval party. But the few remaining sappers had, and there were ropes and other equipment in their gear. Sykes knew he would have to face it. He had come to this realization when the next air strike, at long last, materialized from the west.

Briar had just moved into the enclosed inlet indicated by Morgan, proceeding cautiously through the shallows, when the sound of aircraft engines was picked up. More than one, according to Frome who had come to the bridge to report only minimal damage below.

Cameron said, 'They won't spot us direct. But the Japs are going to report us by light.' It was an uncomfortable feeling to say the least : one small corvette, with a long way to go to make Port Stanley – if ever they got as far even as the Le Maire Strait. But that was for the future : it was a case, as ever, of first things first. Get the landing-party back . . . and for the present an air attack was not likely to be successful. The surrounding land was high, tending in places to overhang the water like the inlet where they had lain up on first arrival. An unlucky chance might get them ; but that was an ordinary hazard of war, as likely in the open sea as here. *Briar* moved on dead slow. When the ship was nicely in, with the sounds above indicating that the aircraft were circling, Cameron brought her up off a shingly, sharply-sloping beach where the new landing-party could get a footing and begin a search for a way up so as to make contact with anyone who was left.

'Stop engines,' he said. *Briar* drifted silently in the night's eeriness. 'All right, Number One. I'll wait till you get back, no time limit. And the best of luck.'

Frome saluted and went down the ladder. His party was already mustered by the seaboat, which was swung out for lowering. Cameron watched them go, a sinking feeling in his guts. So many dead already this night : Carruthers, Fish . . . and God knew what had happened ashore, what Frome was going to find if he found anything at all. War was a bastard, even when you'd deprived the enemy of a cruiser squadron and a flotilla of assault craft, even when you'd carried out your orders to the full. A captain could never escape his conscience.

The Admiralty's operations room was quiet. In London the time was 2300 hours. Quiet, but to some extent fraught ; the Rear Admiral was present with the Duty Captain – and so was the Prime Minister himself. Winston, the Rear-Admiral thought, had never forgotten that he had twice been First Lord of the Admiralty. His interest in the Navy was personal and intense. Tonight the quietness, the lack of movement in the war, bored him, interfered with his enjoyment of his cigar.

'We need some good news, Admiral,' he said.

'We always need that, sir.'

'Yes. We don't always get it! Mind you, the war's not going badly on the whole . . . .' Ruminating, Mr Churchill had dropped off for a catnap when things started happening. A lieutenant-commander entered the operations room with a signal, which he handed to the Rear-Admiral.

'Intercepted transmission from the Japanese carrier off the Magellan Strait, sir.'

'Bloody fools to transmit, what? Might have guessed we'd have broken their cypher.' The Rear-Admiral read, raised his eyebrows, manifested excitement and said, 'Good God! Prime Minister, you wanted good news – ' He broke off, looking irritated, and gestured at the officer who had brought the signal. 'Wake him up, for God's sake – sooner you than me.'

The PM was brought awake with a jerk. The Rear-Admiral got his word in before Mr Churchill could utter. 'Excellent news, sir, from the horse's mouth, the Japanese horse.' He cleared his throat. 'The cruisers *Ichikawa*, *Hakodate* and *Sasebo* with the entire Falklands assault force are immobilized north of Hoste Island –'

'Good heavens!'

'The assault's off, sir. The threat's removed. They'll never get a chance to mount it again.'

The Prime Minister waved his cigar. 'Splendid – splendid! I congratulate all concerned.' He paused. 'We sent a corvette, as I remember. What's the word of her, Admiral?'

'The Japanese intention is to seek her out and attack her with aircraft from the carrier, sir. We have no information from *Briar* herself.'

160

'I see. And what, pray, do you propose to do about it?'

The Rear-Admiral shrugged, caught the eye of the Duty Captain. 'Frankly, I see little we can do. So much distance. One small corvette –'

'One small corvette be damned!' The Prime Minister got to his feet, his face pugnacious, his voice a snarl now. 'You have the effrontery . . . a brave Captain, a brave ship's company who have struck a blow for Britain! They are to be succoured, Admiral.'

'But we must be realistic, sir –'

'I give the order myself. The responsibility is not yours. You have some availability of ships and aircraft at Port Stanley – and the threat is removed by this one small ship. You will send a force at once, Admiral, to close the tip of South America at its maximum speed. I would estimate a cruiser could reach the Le Maire Strait in fourteen hours at thirty knots.' The Prime Minister sat down again. 'I shall remain here until I have word that assistance is on the way. I pray it will not arrive too late.'

The men on the cliff top were caught by the stuttering gunfire as the Japanese fighters swooped low above the open ground. They scattered, running blindly in all directions. Leading Seamen Hoggett died, taken right the way up his spine by a burst of machine-gun fire. Two of the sappers were almost blown over the cliff as the bullets thudded into them. The rest died soon after, as the aircraft came in again and again, taking their revenge for all that had happened. Sykes' body lay like Hoggett's with a line of holes peppering the chest and the head shattered. It was a clean sweep of all but one man: Ordinary Seaman Beaner, who had managed to find the safety of a lump of rock and who squirmed around it, keeping it between himself and the zooming aircraft, managing by some miracle to remain alive and unhurt until the attack withdrew. He lay for some while, sobbing, terrified that they would be back.

161

But they had gone now. It penetrated Beaner's mind that there was a limit to their fuel capacity and he had a respite, he didn't know how long for. He believed they would come back to kill him in due course, after refuelling aboard the carrier out at sea.

He had to get away ; get anywhere before that happened.

He came out from cover, face twisted, and ran. Just ran ; any direction at all. A case of panic . . . and he stumbled into a sort of slide, a place of sharp rubble that went steeply downwards. His instinct for self-preservation enabled him to check his speed at the sacrifice of his flesh. It was a long way down ; when he reached the bottom and rolled towards the water he was alive but his clothing was in shreds and he was as skinned as a rabbit ready for the pot. But he was conscious. He heard voices, dimly saw forms coming towards him, recognized his shipmates, recognized Jimmy the One who took him in his arms and cradled his head.

'All right, Beaner. It's all right now. We'll get you back to the ship.' Frome asked the question, dreading the answer. 'What about the others, Beaner ? The landing-party, the sappers – all of them. Tell me how to reach them, Beaner, for God's sake !'

'They're all dead. Every bloody one, all dead. The aircraft . . . and the cruisers earlier, what got the Major . . . all bloody dead, I tell you. Oh God get me out of this war . . . ' Then Beaner began screaming, screaming without cease as his skinned body trembled as though it would never stop.

Cameron's face was grey when Frome made his report. Bad news piled up. But he had to force himself to think of the good news, the basic success of his mission. Many other lives were going to be saved now. He stiffened, brought his shoulders back and said, 'Now we have to get out, Number One. The job's done. The aircraft will be back – we have to shift before they come. The chart shows that this inlet has access direct to the Beagle Channel. We'll take it slow, keeping doggo till next dark. Then move out fast for the Le Maire Strait.'

'Yes, sir,' Frome said, his voice flat. He turned away. They all knew the risks, knew that the Japs wouldn't let up. But the *Briar* was a tiny target and she still had her guns intact and they might make out. Before he left the bridge he turned back and asked, 'Do you think anyone'll send us cover, sir?'

Cameron grinned, his lips a thin, hard line. 'I wouldn't bank on it, Number One. We're not very important, when all's said and done. But we'll do our best.'

Frome nodded. 'We'll do that, all right,' he said, and went down the ladder. Cameron watched him go. He looked dead tired; they were all dead tired but they would have to keep their wits about them for a long while yet. Especially himself; he had to preserve what was left, at least.

'Engine to Slow Ahead, Pilot.'

'Slow Ahead, sir.'

'Wheel five degrees to starboard.'

'Starboard five sir.'

'Midships . . . steady.'

'Steady, sir,' the coxswain repeated from the wheelhouse. 'Course, oh-eight-nine, sir.'

'Steer oh-nine-oh.'

'Steer oh-nine-oh, sir.' The old routine. The coxswain lit a cigarette and blew smoke. Steer east and get to buggery out of it, don't think too much about the dead left behind in this stinking, frozen waste. It had been quite a night . . . and tomorrow was another day. After that, another if they were lucky. And if they got through this lot, they'd be back at it again somewhere else, maybe in some other ship. Slog away, face danger, war without end.

Away north in the Admiralty, the Prime Minister, now satisfied that everything possible was being done, lumbered off at last to bed.

163